Aman Chiu 著

圖像
速學英語數詞

Learn numbers in English
through pictures

商務印書館

圖像速學英語數詞

Learn numbers in English through pictures

作　　者：Aman Chiu

責任編輯：黃家麗

封面設計：楊愛文

出　　版：商務印書館 (香港) 有限公司

　　　　　香港筲箕灣耀興道 3 號東滙廣場 8 樓

　　　　　http://www.commercialpress.com.hk

發　　行：香港聯合書刊物流有限公司

　　　　　香港新界大埔汀麗路 36 號中華商務印刷大廈 3 字樓

印　　刷：美雅印刷製本有限公司

　　　　　九龍官塘榮業街 6 號海濱工業大廈 4 樓 A 室

版　　次：2015 年 9 月第 1 版第 1 次印刷

　　　　　© 2015 商務印書館 (香港) 有限公司

　　　　　ISBN 978 962 07 1938 7

　　　　　Printed in Hong Kong

目錄
CONTENTS

Section 1: The Basics of Numbers

數詞基本知識

01 CARDINAL NUMBERS 基數詞

基數詞用來表示人、事物數量的多少。我們日常接觸到的基本數字，就是用阿拉伯數字 * 來表示數量 (quantity) 的基數詞。

1.1 怎樣用
Usage

A 0至9的基數詞

基數詞	寫法	讀音	注意
0	zero 零	[zˈɪərou]	也唸 nought 或 O（讀作 oh） 不要把 /z/ 和 /r/ 錯讀為 /s/ 和 /l/
1	one 一	[wʌn]	發音同 won
2	two 二	[tuː]	
3	three 三	[θriː]	不要把 /θ/ 錯讀為 /f/ 或 /fr/
4	four 四	[fɔː]	
5	five 五	[faɪv]	
6	six 六	[sɪks]	
7	seven 七	[ˈsev(ə)n]	不要把 /v/ 錯讀為 /f/
8	eight 八	[eɪt]	發音同 ate，不是 egg
9	nine 九	[naɪn]	不要把第一個 /n/ 錯讀為 /l/

* 阿拉伯數字是現在國際通用的數字（即 1、2、3……），由古代印度人發明，後來經由阿拉伯人傳入歐洲，故被歐洲人誤稱為阿拉伯數字。

用途

1) 認識了基本數字單位，便可表達簡單的數字資訊，如電話、門牌、房間、證件、車牌等號碼。

> **例**
> - 1838 （讀：one eight three eight）
> - Room 1326 （讀：Room one three two six）1326 室
> - Bus route 54 （讀：Bus route fifty four）54 號巴士

如號碼中有重複數字，則用 double 表示。

> **例**
> - 1883 1133 （讀：one double eight three double one double three）

2) 0 一般唸成 zero。在日常會話中，英國人有時會讀作 nought 或 O（讀 oh）。

> **例**
> - 0.6 （讀：nought point six）
> - 1.03 （讀：one point oh three）

※ 注意，美國人在以上所有場合都會使用 zero。

3) 基數詞一般是單數形式，但於下列情況常用複數：

在一些表示 "一排" 或 "一組" 的詞組裏。

> **例**
> - They arrived in twos and threes. 他們三三兩兩的到達了。

在乘法運算的一種標記法裏。

> **例**
> - Three fives are fifteen. 3 x 5 = 15

在固定詞組裏。

> **例**
> - The triple sixes (666) 代表撒旦（魔鬼）
> - The triple sevens (777) 代表上帝（神）

✛ 中英文比較

1）中文的基數詞和英語的情況基本相同，同樣是用來表示人、事物數量的多少，例如：上天賜給我們七十年的壽命。（林語堂《與塵世結不解緣》）/ 香港由港島、大嶼山、九龍半島及新界（包括 262 個離島）組成。

2）中文裏的數詞必須通過量詞才能修飾名詞，而英語中則沒有這個必要，例如：one bed（一張牀）/ two cars（兩輛汽車）/ three horses（三匹馬）/ four bridges（四座橋）和 five buildings（五棟大樓）。又如：沿着荷塘，是一條曲折的小煤屑路。（朱自清《荷塘月色》）古語、諺語、慣用語等則屬例外，例如：四書五經 / 七手八腳 / 一花一世界，一葉一菩提。

3）中文裏，阿拉伯數字用於計量、編號、產品型號、日期等，以突出簡潔醒目的表達效果，如 65%、100 公斤、300 公尺、彌敦道 188 號、28 樓、4G 手機、G8 峰會、1997 年 7 月 1 日等。

10至19的基數詞

除了 10、11、12 之外，基數詞 13 至 19 是由個位數詞的詞幹（stem）後加字尾
（suffix）-teen 構成。

基數詞	寫法	讀音	注意
10	ten 十	[ten]	
11	eleven 十一	[ɪˈlev(ə)n]	
12	twelve 十二	[twelv]	
13	thirteen 十三	[ˈθɜːtiːn]	不規則變化：three + teen → thirteen 不要與 thirty 的發音混淆
14	fourteen 十四	[ˌfɔː(r)ˈtiːn]	
15	fifteen 十五	[ˌfɪfˈtiːn]	不規則變化：five + teen → fifteen
16	sixteen 十六	[ˌsɪksˈtiːn]	
17	seventeen 十七	[ˌsev(ə)nˈtiːn]	
18	eighteen 十八	[ˌeɪˈtiːn]	不規則變化： eight + teen → eighteen
19	nineteen 十九	[ˌnaɪnˈtiːn]	

用途

1) 注意，13、15 和 18 出現不規則變化：

- 13 = three + teen → thirteen
- 15 = five + teen → fifteen
- 18 = eight + teen → eighteen

2) 歐美文化中認為 13 是不祥數。

> **例** • He wouldn't have thirteen guests at his party because it's supposed to be an unlucky number.
> 他不願看見有十三個客人來參加他的聚會，
> 因為十三被認為是個不吉利的數字。

3) dozen（打）為集合數詞（collective number），是數字 12 的另一種表示方法，也是一種計算單位。

> **例** • a / one dozen eggs 一打雞蛋(= 12 eggs) / two dozen eggs
> 兩打雞蛋（24 為 two dozen，不作 two dozens）
> • These eggs are $10 a half dozen. (= $10 for six)
> 這些雞蛋十塊錢半打。

⊕ 中英文比較

歐美文化中認為 13 是不祥數，《聖經》中記載耶穌和其十二門徒吃最後的晚餐時有 13 人，而猶大是在 13 號星期五那天背叛耶穌，所以後來若是 13 日的星期五，便稱之為黑色星期五，被認為是最凶的一天。中國文化中沒有這個忌諱，明朝時有「十三太保」，清朝時有「廣州十三行」，而在廣東話中，它因與「實生」諧音，所以還有吉祥之意，「十三么」更是麻將遊戲中的好牌。

20至99的基數詞

基數詞 20 至 90 是在十位數詞後面加 -ty 構成。

基數詞	寫法	讀音	注意
20	twenty 二十	['twenti]	
30	thirty 三十	['θɜː(r)ti]	不規則變化：three + ty → thirty 不要與 thirteen 的發音混淆
40	forty 四十	['fɔː(r)ti]	不要寫成 fourty（刪 u）
50	fifty 五十	['fɪfti]	不規則變化：five + ty → fifty
60	sixty 六十	['sɪksti]	
70	seventy 七十	['sev(ə)nti]	
80	eighty 八十	['eɪti]	不規則變化：eight + ty → eighty
90	ninety 九十	['naɪnti]	不要寫成 ninty（e 不刪去）

用途

1) 基數詞 21 至 99 是在十位數詞後面加上個位數詞合成，中間加上連字符 (-)。

- 21 = 20 + 1 → twenty-one
- 48 = 40 + 8 → forty-eight
- 65 = 60 + 5 → sixty-five
- 99 = 90 + 9 → ninety-nine

2) 基數詞一般都以單數形式出現，但 twenty、thirty 等常用複數形式用來表示年代或年齡的概數。

- The war broke out in the forties. 戰爭在四十年代爆發。
- He got married in his sixties. 他六十多歲結婚。

3) 英語中表示 20 的集合數詞為 score。

- a score of policemen 二十個警察
- The days of our years are three score years and ten; and if by reason of strength they be four score years. (Psalm 90:10)
  我們一生的年日是七十歲，若是強壯可到八十歲。
  （詩篇第 90 篇 10 節）

4) 英語中的 seventy-eight (78) 除了是基數詞以外，還指「每分鐘 78 轉的舊式唱片」，即廣東話所說的「黑膠唱片」。

- a collection of 78s 一批黑膠唱片收藏品

5) fifty-fifty 是由兩個基數詞組成的慣用語，指「均分；各負一半責任」。

- Let's go fifty-fifty. 讓我們平攤費用吧。
- There's a fifty-fifty chance that I'll succeed.
  我有一半的成功機會。

D　100及以上的基數詞

英語有一套以百（hundred）、千（thousand）、百萬（million）和億萬（billion）來處理較大數字的系統。

基數詞	寫法	讀音 / 注意
100	a / one hundred 一百	['hʌndrəd]
1,000	a / one thousand 一千	['θaʊz(ə)nd]
10,000	ten thousand 一萬	
100,000	a / one hundred thousand 十萬	
1,000,000	a / one million 一百萬	['mɪljən]
10,000,000	ten million 一千萬	
100,000,000	a / one hundred million 一億	
1,000,000,000	a / one thousand million（英式）or a / one billion 十億（美式）	

用途

1) 100 以上的數量通常以數字寫出。

 • There were 133 passengers on the plane. 航班上有 133 名乘客。

• In total, there are about 2,700 different species of snakes around the world. 世界各地總共約有 2,700 種蛇。

2) 如要讀出或寫出數目，必須用 and 帶出最後兩個數字位。

 • 106 = 100 + 06 → one hundred and six

• 333 = 300 + 33 → three hundred and thirty-three

• 989 = 900 + 89 → nine hundred and eighty-nine

※ 注意，美式英語多省略 and。

3) 大於 999 的數位，採用三位分節法，節與節之間用半個字位的空間或逗號隔開。

 • 1 000 / 1,000

• 99 999 / 99,999

• 3 000 000 / 3,000,000

4) 在通俗用法中，"千" 有時可轉換成以 "百" 為單位的方式表達。

 • fifteen hundred (i.e. 1,500) 一千五百

5) 只要掌握用英語表達 1 至 1,000 的讀法和寫法，再大的數字讀法也不難掌握。

三個 0 代表 thousand（1,000 / 千）。

• 1,340	one thousand, three hundred and forty
• 6,833	six thousand, eight hundred and thirty-three
• 60,674	sixty thousand, six hundred and seventy-four
• 999,989	nine hundred and ninety-nine thousand, nine hundred and eighty-nine

六個 0 代表 million（1,000,000 / 百萬）。

- 3,333,333　　　three million, three hundred and thirty-three thousand, three hundred and thirty-three

九個 0 代表 billion（1,000,000,000 / 十億）。

- 9,876,543,210　nine billion, eight hundred and seventy-six million, five hundred and forty-three thousand, two hundred and ten

6) hundred, thousand, million 等數詞前面，若有基數詞或某些表示數量的形容詞時，不加複數 (-s)。

- a few hundred miles 幾百公里 (not a few hundreds)
- two thousand people 兩千人 (not two thousands)
- several million dollars 數百萬元 (not several millions)

此外，切勿在以上詞組中加上介詞 of。

- ✗ a few hundred of miles
- ✗ two thousand of people
- ✗ several million of dollars

7) 但如表示 "幾百"、"幾千"、"幾百萬" 等籠統數目時，則可用上複數 (-s) 加上 of 構成短語（限定詞）。

- I've read it hundreds of times. 我讀過它好幾百次。
- thousands of books 幾千本書
- millions of miles of highway 數以百萬公里的高速公路

也可單獨作代名詞用。

- (Newspaper headline) Thousands Killed in Earthquake.
  [新聞標題] 地震中數千人遇難

8) 大於 "一百億億"（trillion）的數位通常用在天文學的計算中，一般情況非常罕見，需要表達時，通常採用 10 若干次方的方式，即 10 之後若干個零。

- ten to the power sixteen / ten to the sixteen (power)
  10 的 16 次方（即：10 000 000 000 000 000）

⊕ **中英文比較**

英語不像中文有萬、十萬、千萬、億這樣的單位數詞，而是採用三位分節法，例如一萬用「10 千（ten thousand）」來表示，十萬用「100 千（a hundred thousand）」來表示，千萬用「10 百萬（ten million）」來表示，億則用「100 百萬（a hundred million）」來表示。

 ## 1.2 速查表
Speed check

基數詞對照表

1	One	
10	Ten	
100	Hundred	
1,000	One	Thousand
10,000	Ten	Thousand
100,000	Hundred	Thousand
1,000,000	One	Million
10,000,000	Ten	Million
100,000,000	Hundred	Million
1,000,000,000	One	Billion
10,000,000,000	Ten	Billion
100,000,000,000	Hundred	Billion
1,000,000,000,000	One	Trillion
10,000,000,000,000	Ten	Trillion
100,000,000,000,000	Hundred	Trillion

02 ORDINAL NUMBERS 序數詞

另一套數學上以排序（order）為主的數字系列稱為序數詞，它們用來表示人、事物排列的先後次序。

 ## 2.1 怎樣用
Usage

A 1至9的序數詞

除了 first、second、third 三個特別情況之外，以下所有序數詞都是由基數詞加上字尾（suffix）-th 而組成，但個別例子會出現不規則變化。

序數詞	寫法	讀音	注意
1st	first 第一	[fɜː(r)st]	
2nd	second 第二	['sek(ə)nd]	
3rd	third 第三	[θɜː(r)d]	
4th	fourth 第四	[fɔː(r)θ]	
5th	fifth 第五	[fɪfθ]	不規則變化：five + th → fifth
6th	sixth 第六	[sɪksθ]	
7th	seventh 第七	['sev(ə)nθ]	
8th	eighth 第八	[eɪtθ]	不規則變化：eight + th → eighth
9th	ninth 第九	[naɪnθ]	不規則變化：nine + th → ninth

※注意，序數用作排列，沒有0的存在。

用途

1) 序數詞是用來表示順序及等級。

- He always likes to sit in the first row. 他總愛坐在最前的那一行。
- He came third in English. 他英語科考第三名。
- Jupiter is the fifth planet from the Sun.
  木星是太陽系從內向外的第五顆行星。

2) 序數詞的簡稱用於表示日期。

- I was born on August 8th.
  （讀：August the eighth 或 the eighth of August）
  我在八月八日出生。

3) 序數詞作修飾語（modifier）用。

- the first two pages　前兩頁
- the second half　下半
- 9th grade maths worksheets　第九班數學工作紙

4) 序數詞作代詞（pronoun）用。

- I have two questions. The first is 'Where's my wallet?'
  The second is 'Who stole my money?'
  我有兩個問題，第一，"我的錢包在哪兒？"
  第二，"誰偷了我的錢？"
- Calvin is the third of four sons.　凱文在四名兄弟中排第三。

5) 常見含序數詞的慣用語包括：

- the First Lady　第一夫人
- at first　起初
- at first sight　初次看見時
- second to none　首屈一指的
- on second thoughts　再考慮
- fifth column　（從事秘密活動協助敵軍的）第五縱隊

➕ 中英文比較

中文通常在基數詞前面加「第」、「初」等詞來構成序數詞，表示在系列中的次序和位置，例如：第一（the first）、第二場（the second scene / Scene 2）、初三（the third day of a lunar month）等。其他形式還有「數詞＋名詞」，例如：（某月）六號（the sixth of (a month)）、十八樓（the eighteenth floor）、三嫂（sister-in-law / one's third older brother's wife）、五叔（uncle / one's father's fifth younger brother）、卷十二（the twelve volume）、頭一回（the first time）、最後一次（the last time）等。

B　10至19的序數

序數	寫法	讀音	注意
10th	tenth 第十	[tenθ]	
11th	eleventh 第十一	[ɪˈlev(ə)nθ]	
12th	twelfth 第十二	[twelfθ]	不規則變化：twelve + th = twelfth
13th	thirteenth 第十三	[ˌθɜː(r)ˈtiːnθ]	不要與 thirtieth 的發音混淆
14th	fourteenth 第十四	[ˌfɔː(r)ˈtiːnθ]	不要寫成 forteenth（u 不刪去）
15th	fifteenth 第十五	[ˌfɪfˈtiːnθ]	
16th	sixteenth 第十六	[ˌsɪksˈtiːnθ]	
17th	seventeenth 第十七	[ˌsev(ə)nˈtiːnθ]	不要把 /v/ 錯讀為 /f/
18th	eighteenth 第十八	[ˌeɪˈtiːnθ]	
19th	nineteenth 第十九	[ˌnaɪnˈtiːnθ]	不要把第一個 /n/ 錯讀為 /l/ 不要寫成 ninteenth（e 不刪去）

用途

1) 同樣，這組序數詞也是用來表示順序及等級。

 • I live on the 17th floor. 我住在十七樓。
   • The 2016 race will mark the 18th Standard Chartered Marathon.
   2016 年的賽事將會標誌着渣打馬拉松進入第十八年。

2) 序數詞的簡稱用於表示日期或年代。

 • in the 19th century 在十九世紀
   • Technology, science, and inventions have progressed at an
   accelerated rate during the hundred years of the 20th century,
   more so than any other century. 二十世紀的一百年間，科技、
   科學以至各項發明均取得一日千里之發展，此等發展速度為
   以往世紀所前所未見的。

3) 序數詞常見於週年紀念。

 • 12th anniversary celebration 十二週年紀念慶祝
   • Commemorate your 15th wedding anniversary with a
   traditional gift of crystal. 以傳統水晶飾物慶賀閣下結婚十五週
   年紀念。

20至99的序數

這組序數同樣是由基數加上字尾 -th 所組成，但同時出現不規則變化，即是把詞尾 -y 轉成 -ie，再加上 -th 而組成。

序數	寫法	讀音	注意
20th	twentieth 第二十	['twentiəθ]	
30th	thirtieth 第三十	['θɜː(r)tiəθ]	不要與 thirteenth 的發音混淆
40th	fortieth 第四十	['fɔː(r)tiəθ]	不要寫成 fourtieth（刪 u）
50th	fiftieth 第五十	['fɪftiəθ]	
60th	sixtieth 第六十	['sɪkstiəθ]	
70th	seventieth 第七十	['sev(ə)ntiəθ]	
80th	eightieth 第八十	['eɪtiəθ]	
90th	ninetieth 第九十	['naɪntiəθ]	不要寫成 ninty（e 不刪去）

用途

1) 認識了以上八個序數，21 至 99 的序數說法就簡單得多。

- 21 = 20 + 1st → twenty-first
- 32 = 30 + 2nd → thirty-second
- 53 = 50 + 3rd → fifty-third
- 75 = 70 + 5th → seventy-fifth
- 99 = 90 + 9th → ninety-ninth

2) 這組序數詞多見於與週年紀念有關的上下文中。

- It's grandma's 88th birthday today. 今天是祖母 88 歲大壽。
- Apple's TAM was a limited-edition computer that was released in 1997 in celebration of the company's 20th birthday.
  1997 年推出的 TAM 是蘋果為紀念公司成立 20 週年而推出的紀念版電腦。

結婚週年有一套特定的名稱。

- Wedding gifts vary in different countries, but some years have well-established connections now common to most nations: 15th Crystal, 20th China, 25th Silver, 30th Pearl, 40th Ruby, 50th Golden, 60th Diamond. 結婚禮物因國而異，但大部份國家已有一套約定俗成的規矩：15 週年水晶婚，20 週年陶瓷婚，25 週年銀婚，30 週年珍珠婚，40 週年紅寶石婚，50 週年金婚以及 60 週年鑽石婚。

100及以上的序數

下面是序數 100（百）、1,000（千）、10,000（萬）、100,000（十萬）、1,000,000（百萬）、10,000,000（千萬）、100,000,000（億）和 1,000,000,000（十億）的簡稱及英語全寫。

序數	寫法	讀音
100th	a / one hundredth 第一百	['hʌndrədθ]
1,000th	a / one thousandth 第一千	['θaʊz(ə)nθ]
10,000th	ten thousandth 第一萬	
100,000th	a / one hundred thousandth 第十萬	
1,000,000th	a / one millionth 第一百萬	['mɪljənθ]
10,000,000th	ten millionth 第一千萬	
100,000,000th	a / one hundred millionth 第一億	
1,000,000,000th	a / one thousand millionth or a / one billionth 第十億	

用途

由於英語序數和基數都是在最後一個單字才有分別，只要掌握到用英語表達序數 1st 至 1,000th 的手法，其餘的序數有多大數值也不難應付。

- 2012th → two thousand and twelfth
- 9,876,543,210th → nine billion, eight hundred and seventy-six million, five hundred and forty-three thousand, two hundred and tenth

2.2 速查表
Speed check

序數對照表

1ˢᵗ	First
2ⁿᵈ	Second
3ʳᵈ	Third
4ᵗʰ	Fourth
5ᵗʰ	Fifth
6ᵗʰ	Sixth
7ᵗʰ	Seventh
8ᵗʰ	Eighth
9ᵗʰ	Ninth
10ᵗʰ	Tenth
11ᵗʰ	Eleventh
12ᵗʰ	Twelfth
13ᵗʰ	Thirteenth
14ᵗʰ	Fourteenth
15ᵗʰ	Fifteenth
16ᵗʰ	Sixteenth
17ᵗʰ	Seventeenth
18ᵗʰ	Eighteenth
19ᵗʰ	Nineteenth
20ᵗʰ	Twentieth
21ˢᵗ	Twenty-first
22ⁿᵈ	Twenty-second
23ʳᵈ	Twenty-third
30ᵗʰ	Thirtieth
40ᵗʰ	Fortieth
50ᵗʰ	Fiftieth
60ᵗʰ	Sixtieth
70ᵗʰ	Seventieth
80ᵗʰ	Eightieth
90ᵗʰ	Ninetieth
100ᵗʰ	Hundredth
101ˢᵗ	Hundred and first
200ᵗʰ	Two hundredth
1,000ᵗʰ	Thousandth
10,000ᵗʰ	Ten thousandth
100,000ᵗʰ	One hundred thousandth
1,000,000ᵗʰ	One millionth

03 ROMAN NUMERALS 羅馬數字

羅馬數字起源於羅馬,是最早的數字表示方式,它是歐洲在阿拉伯數字傳入之前使用的一種數碼,它的產生標誌着一種古代文明的進步。

3.1 怎樣用
Usage

A 1至10的羅馬數字

羅馬數字只有 7 個基本字符:I(1)、V(5)、X(10)、L(50)、C(100)、D(500)、M(1,000)。 數值 1 至 10 由 I、V、X 三個字符組合而成。

羅馬數字	數值	拉丁	說明
I	1	Uno	古羅馬人用手指作計算工具,為了表示一、二、三、四個物體,就分別伸出一、二、三、四隻手指。
II	2	Duo	
III	3	Tres	
IV	4	Quattuor	由於 IV 是古羅馬神話主神朱比特的首字,為了避諱,有時用 IIII 代替 IV。
V	5	Quinque	表示五個物體就伸出一隻手,寫成 V 形,表示大指與食指張開的形狀。
VI	6	Sex	
VII	7	Septem	
VIII	8	Octo	
IX	9	Novem	
X	10	Decem	表示十個物體就伸出兩隻手,畫成 VV 形,後來寫成一隻手向上,一隻手向下的 X。

※ 注意,羅馬數字中沒有 0。一般認為羅馬數字只用來記數,而不作演算。

用途

1) 所有數值均按照「連寫」和「右加左減」的規則組合而成。

連寫：相同的數字連寫，所表示的數等於這些數字相加得到的數。

- II = 1 + 1 = 2
- III = 1 + 1 + 1 = 3

※ 注意，連寫數字最多為三位，但 4 屬於例外，既然可寫成 IV，又可寫作 IIII。

右加：小的數字在大的數字的右邊，所表示的數等於這些數字相加得到的數。

- VI = 5 + 1 = 6
- VII = 5 + 2 = 7
- VIII = 5 + 3 = 8
- XV = 10 + 5 = 15
- XXIII = 20 + 3 = 23

※ 注意，右加數字最多為三位，比如 9 寫成 IX，而非 VIIII。

左減：小的數字在大的數字的左邊，所表示的數等於大數減小數得到的數。

- IV = 5 - 1 = 4
- IX = 10 - 1 = 9

※ 注意，V 和 X 左邊的小數字只能用 I。左減數字必須為一位，比如 8 不能寫成 IIX (10 - 1 - 1)，而右加的數字最多可以是三位，所以 8 必須寫成 VIII (5 + 1 + 1 + 1)。

11至100的羅馬數字

為了表示較大的數，古羅馬人用拉丁字 centum（century）的頭一個字母 C 表示一百，另取字母 C 的一半，成為符號 L，表示五十。

羅馬數字	數值	羅馬數字	數值
XI	11	XLI	41
XII	12	XLIII	43
XIII	13	XLV	45
XIV	14	XLIX	49
XV	15	**L**	**50**
XVI	16	LII	52
XVII	17	LV	55
XVIII	18	LVI	56
XIX	19	LVIII	58
XX	20	LX	60
XXI	21	LXI	61
XXIV	24	LXVI	66
XXVI	26	LXX	70
XXVIII	28	LXXIV	74
XXX	30	LXXX	80
XXXII	32	LXXXV	85
XXXV	35	XC	90
XXXVII	37	XCIII	93
XXXIX	39	XCIX	99
XL	40	**C**	**100**

用途

1) 認識了數值 1 至 10 的表示方法，便可自行組成更大的數值。

連寫：

 ・X X　　= 10 + 10 = 20
・X XX　= 10 + 10 + 10 = 30

※ 注意，連寫數字最多為三位，比如 40 寫成 XL（50 - 10），而非 XXXX（10+10+10+10）。

右加：

 ・XI　　　= 10 + 1 = 11
・XXII　　= 20 + 2 = 22
・XXXIII = 30 + 3 = 33
・XLIV　 = 40 + 4 = 44
・LIX　　 = 50 + 9 = 59

※ 注意，右加數字最多為三位，比如 90 寫成 XC (100-10)，而非 LXXXX（50+10+10+10+10）。

左減：L 和 C 左邊的小數字只能用 X。

 ・IX　　= 10 - 1 = 9
・XL　　= 50 - 10 = 40
・XC　　= 100 - 10 = 90

※ 注意，左減的數字有限制，僅限於 I、X、C。比如 45 不可以寫成 VL（50 - 5），只能是 XLV（40 + 5）。

左減時也不可跨越一個位數。比如 99 不可以寫成 IC（100 - 1），而是用 XCIX（[100 - 10] + [10 - 1] = 90 + 9 = 99）表示。

100以上的羅馬數字

為了表示更大的數，古羅馬人用拉丁字 Mille 的頭一個字母 M 表示一千。另取字母 D 表示五百。

羅馬數字	數值
C	100
CI	101
CXXV	125
CL	150
CC	200
CXXX	230
CCC	300
CCCLXXX	380
CD	400
D	500
DC	600
DCC	700
DCCC	800
CM	900
M	1000
MDC	1600
MDCC	1700
MCM	1900
MM	2000
MMXV	2015

用途

1) 按照上節所述規則可以表示任何正整數。

連寫：

- CC   = 100 + 100 = 200
- CCC   = 100 + 100 + 100 = 300
- MM   = 1,000 + 1,000 = 2,000
- MMM   = 1,000 + 1,000 + 1,000 = 3,000

※ 注意，同一數碼最多只能出現三次，如 400 不可表示為 CCCC，而要表示為 CD（500 - 100）。

右加：

- CL   = 100 + 50 = 150
- DXCIX = 500 + 99 = 599

左減：D 和 M 左邊的小數字只能用 C。

- CD   = 500 – 100 = 400
- CM   = 1,000 – 100 = 900

2) 大於 5,000 的數字則以「加線乘千」法表示。

在一個數的上面畫一條橫線，表示這個數增值 1,000 倍。

- $\overline{\text{V}}$ = 5 x 1,000 = 5,000
- $\overline{\text{XII}}$ = 12 x 1,000 = 12,000

如果上方有兩條橫線，即是原數的 1,000,000（1000^2）倍。

- $\overset{==}{\text{XII}}$ = 12 x 1,000 x 1,000 = 12,000,000

羅馬數字的用途

羅馬數字因書寫繁難，除了用於以下情況，後人已很少採用。

1) 用於歷代君主及教宗的冠名上。

- Henry VIII　　　　　亨利八世(英國都鐸王朝第二任國王)
- Louis XIV　　　　　路易十四 (法國波旁王朝國王)
- Elizabeth II　　　　伊利沙伯二世(現任英國女皇)
- Pope Benedict XVI　教宗本篤十六世(前任教宗)

2) 雕刻於公共紀念建築物、紀念碑或墓碑上以表示年份，予人古雅莊重的氣氛。

3) 用於日曆或鐘錶，以營造典雅氣息。

- Why does the Roman numeral for 4 on watches and clocks read IIII instead of the correct manner, IV? 為甚麼鐘錶上代表 4 的羅馬數字會寫成 IIII，而不是正確的寫法 IV ？

(注：IIII 這種記號源於 14 世紀，當時法國國王查理五世下令不准用 IV，據說是因為 IV 與古羅馬神話中眾神之王朱庇特 (Jupiter) 的拉丁文拼寫 IVPPITER 有雷同之處，所以必須有所避諱，改 IV 為 IIII。)

4) 用於紀年的裝飾設計 (例如婚戒) 或紋身圖案，例如英國球星大衛・碧咸 / 貝克漢姆 (David Beckham) 右手臂上紋有的羅馬數字 VII，是用來紀念他效力曼聯時的輝煌戰績，當時他身穿 7 號戰袍，為曼聯奪得多次英超與足總冠軍。又例如加拿大小天王賈斯汀比伯 (Justin Bieber) 的右胸前紋有 I、IX、VII、V 四個羅馬數字，代表 1975，這是他敬愛的母親的出生年份。

5) 用於電影或電視節目製作年份，例如 TVB 在節目最後播出之台徽畫面的右下角總會打出羅馬數字的字樣，如 MCMXCVII（1997），代表該節目的製作年份。又如：

- Copyright © MMXVI CBS, Inc. All Rights Reserved
  版權所有 哥倫比亞廣播公司 2016

6) 書籍、文件的章節編號或戲劇的分幕分場等。

例
- Chapter XXII 第二十二章
- Section V.4 第五段之第四節
- Act II, Scene V 第二幕第五場

※ 注意，圖書的扉頁（指在書籍封面或襯頁之後、正文之前的頁數）常以羅馬數字的小寫字母來表示（即 i、ii、iii、iv、v 等）。

3.2 速查表
Speed check

羅馬數字對照表

I	1	XXXI	31	LXI	61	LXXI	91
II	2	XXXII	32	LXII	62	LXXII	92
III	3	XXXIII	33	LXIII	63	LXXIII	93
IV	4	XXXIV	34	LXIV	64	LXXIV	94
V	**5**	XXXV	35	LXV	65	LXXV	95
VI	6	XXXVI	36	LXVI	66	LXXVI	96
VII	7	XXXVII	37	LXVII	67	LXXVII	97
VIII	8	XXXVIII	38	LXVIII	68	LXXVIII	98
IX	9	XXXIX	39	LXIX	69	LXXIX	99
X	**10**	XL	40	LXX	70	**C**	**100**
XI	11	XLI	41	LXXI	71	**D**	**500**
XII	12	XLII	42	LXXII	72	**M**	**1000**
XIII	13	XLIII	43	LXXIII	73		
XIV	14	XLIV	44	LXXIV	74		
XV	15	XLV	45	LXXV	75		
XVI	16	XLVI	46	LXXVI	76		
XVII	17	XLVII	47	LXXVII	77		
XVIII	18	XLVIII	48	LXXVIII	78		
XIX	19	XLIX	49	LXXIX	79		
XX	20	**L**	**50**	LXXX	80		
XXI	21	LI	51	LXI	81		
XXII	22	LII	52	LXII	82		
XXIII	23	LIII	53	LXIII	83		
XXIV	24	LIV	54	LXIV	84		
XXV	25	LV	55	LXV	85		
XXVI	26	LVI	56	LXVI	86		
XXVII	27	LVII	57	LXVII	87		
XXVIII	28	LVIII	58	LXVIII	88		
XXIX	29	LIX	59	LXIX	89		
XXX	30	LX	60	LXX	90		

04 FRACTIONS 份數

fraction 為數學名詞，來自拉丁語 fractus，意指 broken，用來表示一個單位幾份之幾的數。

4.1 怎樣用
Usage

<table>
<tr><th>A</th><th>基本份數</th></tr>
</table>

份數中間的一條橫線叫做份數線，份數線上面的數叫做份子（numerator），份數線下面的數叫做份母（denominator）。

份數	讀法	圖示
$1/2$	a [one] half 二份之一；一半	
$1/3$	one third 三份之一	
$1/4$	a [one] quarter 四份之一	
$1/5$	a [one] fifth 五份之一	
$1/6$	a [one] sixth 六份之一	
$1/7$	a [one] seventh 七份之一	
$1/8$	an [one] eighth 八份之一	
$1/9$	a [one] ninth 九份之一	
$1/10$	a [one] tenth 十份之一	

用途

1) 用英語表達份數，常借助於基數詞和序數詞。基數詞表示份子，序數詞表示份母。

   - ⅓   a / one third 三份之一
   - ¼   a / one fourth; a / one quarter 四份之一

   ※ 注意，½ 通常讀作 a [one] half，不讀作 a second。¼ 可以說 one fourth，但更常用 a quarter 來表示。

2) 份子大於 1 時，份母（序數詞）要用複數。

   - ⅖   two fifths 五份之二
   - ⅔   two thirds 三份之二
   - ¾   three quarters 四份之三

   ※ 注意，¾ 可以說 three fourths，但常用 three quarters 表示。

3) 帶份數的讀法：在整數與份數之間用 and 連接。

   - 5½   five and a half 五又二份之一
   - 12¾   twelve and three quarters 十二又四份之三

4) 有時為了簡潔起見，份子和份母均可用基數詞讀出，其間用介詞 over。在數學上對於比較複雜的份數通常採用此讀法。

   - ³/₂₆₇   three over two hundred and sixty-seven

5) 若份數在句子中作主語，則謂語動詞是用單數還是複數取決於名詞，即與份數所修飾的名詞保持一致。

   - Only one fifth of air consists of oxygen. 氧氣只佔空氣的五份之一。
   - About one tenth of the students are new immigrants. 大約十份之一的學生是新移民。
   - Only one fourth of the cake was eaten. 只吃掉了四份之一的蛋糕。

6) 帶份數修飾名詞時，該名詞通常是複數。

 • You'd better finish the marathon within one and a fourth **hours**.
你最好在一小時十五分鐘內跑完馬拉松。

7) 但若名詞置於整數 one 或 a 之後，則用單數。

 • The atom breaks up in a **minute** and a quarter. 原子在一分鐘
十五秒內裂變。

8) 最後，請注意份數在電腦可有以下不同寫法。

• ½　1/2　$\frac{1}{2}$　$\dfrac{1}{2}$

✛ 中英文比較

中文的份數以「幾份之幾」來表示，例如：四份之一的世紀，我眼見臺北長高又長大。（余光中《思臺北，念臺北》）/ 世上所謂窮人，百份之九十以上是相對的窮。（王力《窮》）在慣用語裏或份數兼含概數的情況下，「幾份之幾」中的「份」字省去不用，例如：人生不如意事十之八九。/ 曾國藩家書固然有名，其中十之六七是教誨。（張健《家書》）

讀帶份數時須加入「又」字，例如：8½（八又二份之一）、-5¾（負五又四份之三）。

此外，中文的「半」也是份數，例如「大半」、「小半」，又如：他在香港住了兩年半。/ 人過半百是可做壽的。（高行健《花豆》）

古語中讀份母與份子則並無字元區分，例如「其亡者三二」指全體中有三份之二人員死亡。

4.2 速查表
Speed check

份數的寫法和讀法

½	a half / one half 二份之一
⅓	a third / one third 三份之一
¼	a quarter / one quarter; a fourth / one fourth 四份之一
⅕	a fifth / one fifth 五份之一
⅙	a sixth / one sixth 六份之一
⅐	a seventh / one seventh 七份之一
⅛	an eighth / one eighth 八份之一
⅑	a ninth / one ninth 九份之一
⅒	a tenth / one tenth 十份之一
¾	three quarters / three fourths / three over four 四份之三
6½	six and a half 六又二份之一
12³⁄₅	twelve and three fifths 十二又五份之三
²⁰⁄₉₃	twenty over ninety-three 九十三份之二十

DECIMALS AND PERCENTAGES

小數與百份數

小數和百份數是用來表達份數的一種特殊形式。

 ## 5.1 怎樣用
Usage

A 小數

所有份數都可以表示成小數（decimals）。例如 $\frac{1}{10}$ 可以寫成 0.1；$1\frac{1}{4}$ 可以寫 1.25 等。

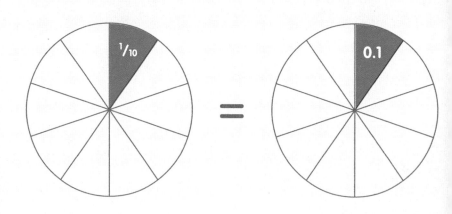

用途

1) 小數是以基數詞加小數點表示。小數點 (.) 的讀法是 point，小數點前面的數，按基數詞的規則讀出，小數點後面的數，按個位基數詞依次讀出。

- 0.5　　　　　zero point five
- 0.006　　　　zero point zero zero six
- 0.257　　　　zero point two five seven
- 1.75　　　　 one point seven five
- 148.06　　　 one hundred and forty-eight point zero six

※ 注意，在英式英語中，其中 zero 可替換為 nought 或讀作 oh。在美式英語則沒有這個變化，0 一律讀作 zero。

2) 所謂按個位基數詞依次讀出小數點後面的數的意思，是指每個數字單獨讀出，而不是作為一個整數讀出。

- 0.257　　× zero point two hundred and fifty seven
　　　　　　✓ nought / zero point two five seven
- 11.603　 × eleven point six hundred and three
　　　　　　✓ eleven point six oh three

3) 小數點前的小數少於 1 時，nought（或 zero）可略去不讀。

- 0.257　　　　point two five seven

4) 小數主要用作定語。

- The current output is 3.2 times that of 2000. 我們現在的糧食產量是 2000 年的 3.2 倍。
- The total output value was up 4.45 times. 總產量提高了 4.45 倍。
- With a population of more than 7.2 million, Hong Kong is one of most densely populated cities in the world. 香港以其七百二十多萬人口躋身於世界人口密度最高的城市之一。

5) 有些數位驟眼看像小數，例如圖書章節、表格、插圖清單等。此等數字並非小數，切勿混淆。

- Table 5.2
- figure 12.3

百份數

所有份數都可以表示成百份數（percentages），例如 ¹/₁₀ 可以寫成 10%；1¼ 可以寫 125% 等。如果用一般份數形式來表示，由於份母不同，不容易看出精確的變化，而百份數的份母都是 100，只要看份子，就能看出數與數之間的明顯差別與變化。因此，百份數在各行各業的生產和生活中，都有着廣泛的應用。

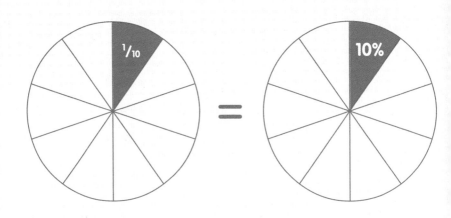

用途

1) 百份數是由基數詞或小數加百份號組成，百份號（%）讀作 percent。

- 0.6%　　　zero point six percent
- 5%　　　　five percent
- 100%　　　one hundred percent
- 12.34%　　twelve point three four percent

※ 注意，數字與百份號之間一般不需留空一格。而 percent 可以是一個單字，也可以分作兩個字來書寫，即 per cent。

2) 日常生活中不少計量單位都以百份數來表示。

 • to charge interest at six percent 收取百份之六的利息
  • humidity of more than 90% 濕度超過 90%
  • Most restaurants have a 10% service charge. 大部份酒樓都會收取百份之十的服務費。

3) 百份數特別用於進行調查、統計、分析、比較時。

 • He won 36.8 percent of the vote. 他贏得了 36.8% 的選票。
  • More than 90 percent of the employees used public transportation. 百份之九十以上的員工使用公共交通。
  • Only 20% of the mice were observed to react to the stimulus. 根據觀察，只有百份之二十的老鼠對刺激有反應。
  • Poland is 90% Roman Catholic. 波蘭九成人是天主教徒。
  • With 90-95 percent of the work complete, we can relax. 九成以上的工作完成了，我們可以放鬆一下。
  • She got 95 percent in Mandarin test. 她在普通話測試中取得 95 分。

4) 也可以與正式統計或分析無關，而純粹表示一種可能。

 • a 100 percent likelihood of winning 百份百的成功機會
  • I was ninety-nine point nine percent sure I was dreaming. (New Moon, Stephenie Meyers) 我百份之九十九的肯定我是在做夢。

5.2 速查表
Speed check

份數與小數、百份數關係表

份數	小數	百份數
1/1	1.0	100%
1/2	0.5	50%
1/3	0.333	33.333%
1/4	0.25	25%
1/5	0.2	20%
1/6	0.1667	16.666%
1/7	0.1429	14.286%
1/8	0.125	12.5%
1/9	0.111	11.111%
1/10	0.1	10%

06 CALCULATIONS 運算

四則運算 (four arithmetic operations)，即加、減、乘、除，是
數學最基本的運算。

6.1 怎樣用
Usage

 加數 (Addition)

用途

1) 數目小的加數，一般用 and 來讀出加號 (+)，例如 What's nine and six? (9 加 6 是多少？)。 等號 (=) 則用 is 或 are 來讀出。

> **例**
> • 2 + 3 = 5
> Two and three are five.
> • 7 + 8 = 15
> Seven and eight is fifteen.

2) 數目相對較大的加數，一般用 plus 來讀出加號 (+)，用 is 或 equals 來讀出等號 (=)。

> **例**
> • 186 + 579 = 765
> One hundred and eighty-six plus five hundred and seventy-nine is / equals seven hundred and sixty-five.

3) 在正式的場合中，不論是大小數目的加數都用 plus 和 is 或 equals。

減數 (Subtraction)

用途

1) 在日常會話中，如數目小的減數，一般用 from 來讀出減號 (-)，用 is 或 leaves 來讀出等號 (=)。

- 8 - 4 = 4
  Four from eight leaves / is four.

  也可讀成：
  - Eight takes away four leaves / is four.

2) 而在正式場合，或數目相對較大的減數，一般用 minus 來讀出減號 (-)，用 equals 來讀出等號 (=)。

- 898 - 333 = 565
  Eight hundred and ninety-eight minus three hundred and thirty-three equals five hundred and sixty-five.

乘數 (Multiplication)

用途

1) 數目小的乘數可直接讀出兩個數位,第二個數位以複數形式讀出, 等號 (=) 以 are 來讀出。

- 2 x 3 = 6
  Two threes are six.
- 7 x 8 = 56
  Seven eights are fifty-six.

2) 數目相對較大的乘數,一般用 times 來讀出 x,用 is 或 makes 來讀 出 =。

- 16 x 125 = 2000
  Sixteen times one hundred and twenty-five **is / makes** two thousand.

3) 正式的場合用 multiplied by 來讀出 x,用 equals 來讀出 =。例如以 上例子會讀作:

- 16 multiplied by 125 equals 2000.

D ## 除數 (Division)

用途

1) 一般用 divided by 來讀出 ÷ ，用 equals 來讀出 = 就可以。

- 18 ÷ 3 = 6
  Eighteen divided by three equals six.
- 2000 ÷ 125 = 16
  Two thousand divided by one hundred and
  twenty-five equals sixteen.

2) 數目很小的除數，有時會用 into 和 goes 來表示。

- 8 ÷ 2 = 4
  Two into eight goes four.

整條乘數的讀法

```
            123
    x       345
    _____

         36 900
          4 920
            615
    _____

         42 435
```

以上整條乘數的讀法如下：

A hundred and twenty-three times three hundred and forty-five.

1   Put down two noughts.

2   Three threes are nine; three twos are six; three ones are three.

3   (Next line) Put down one nought.

4   Four threes are twelve; put down 2 and carry 1; four twos are eight and one are nine; four ones are four.

5   (Next line) Five threes are fifteen; put down 5 and carry 1; five twos are ten and one are eleven; put down 1 and carry 1; five ones are five and one are six.

6   (The addition) Five and nought and nought is five; one and two is three; Two nines are eighteen and six are twenty-four; put down 4 and carry 2, four and six are ten and two are twelve; put down 2 and carry 1; three and one are four.

7   (Total) Forty-two thousand four hundred and thirty-five.

F 倍數的表達方法

1) 用百份比（%）表示。

> 例 • The money supply is 200% up compared with 2000. 貨幣供應與 2000 年相比增長了一倍.

2) 用 …times 表示。

> 例 • Their living room is three times as large as ours. 他們的客廳是我們的三倍大小。

3) 如果表示"是……兩倍數"，一般用 twice。

> 例 • My bedroom is twice as large as yours.
> 我的睡房是你的兩倍大小。

4) 用 -fold 表示。

> 例 • The value of the apartment has increased three-fold. 這套住房的價格已是原先的三倍。

5) 用動詞 double、triple 表示倍數。

> 例 • Sales doubled in three years. 銷售額三年之內增加了一倍。
> • Our company tripled our profits last year. 我們的公司去年的利潤增長了三倍。

6.2 速查表
Speed check

四式運算的讀法

運算	算式	讀法
+	6 + 3 = 9	Six and three are nine.
-	6 - 3 = 3	Three from six leaves three.
X	6 x 3 = 18	Six threes are eighteen.
÷	6 ÷ 3 = 2	Three into six goes two.

07 NUMBERS IN EVERYDAY LIFE

日常生活使用的數字

我們日常接觸到的簡單數字資訊，如電話號碼、證件號碼等，一般以基數表達即可。

7.1 怎樣用

Usage

A 電話號碼

用途

1) 要讀出電話號碼，只要清楚、順序地唸出每個在 0 至 9 以內的數字便可。

    ● 9321 4567
   讀：nine three two one, four five six seven

2) 當同一個數字連續重複出現兩次、三次，便要分別用上 double 和 triple 來避免重複唸讀數字。

    ● 2112 3363
   讀：two double one two, double three six three
   ● 9888 7766
   讀：nine triple eight, double seven double six

3) 寫電話號碼時，一般用括號標示地區號，把電話號碼分節（如兩節）來書寫，以方便讀者清楚掌握數字。比較以下兩種書寫方式：

   例 ● Easy:　（852）8365 7409
   ● Hard:　85283657409

4) 電話號碼中出現 0 這個數字，除了可以把它唸成 zero 之外，也有不少人把它唸作 /əʊ/，即英語字母 O 的發音。

- 2012 2012
  讀：two oh one two, two oh one two
- 9800 7000
  讀：nine eight double oh, seven triple oh

5) 如果你想確認自己沒有撥錯電話號碼，你可以向對方問 Is that + number？

- A: Hello.
  B: Is that 9232 6282?
- A: Er, yes it is.
  B: This is The Commercial Press from Hong Kong.

※ 注意：美國人會說 Is this...?，而不說 Is that...?。
此外，也可乾脆把電話數字用作一個問句讀出。

- A: Hello? 9232 6282?
  B: Yes?

如果對方打錯電話，你可以這樣回答：I think you've got the wrong number.。或乾脆回答說 Sorry, wrong number.。

車牌和信用卡號碼等

除了電話號碼之外，還有其他日常會用到或見到的號碼，例如學生編號、身份證號碼、銀行賬戶號碼、信用卡號碼、登入密碼、車牌號碼等等，用英語表達時的手法也大致相同。

1) 車牌號碼

不少國家及地區都有自訂車輛登記號碼。在香港，此等號碼組合須由英文字母及／或數字組成，總數不得超過 8 個，而三個容易引起混淆的英文字母（I、O 及 Q）不得使用。例如車牌號碼 1 LOVE U，驟眼看是「我愛你」的意思，但其實是由兩個數字加上四個英文字母（one L zero V E U）所組成。

又如國際著名品牌 Chanel 因以其第五號香水（No. 5）馳名於世，所以採用了 N0 5（N zero five）的車牌號碼行走倫敦街頭，以起宣傳之效。

- Number plates have always been a great advertising tool. Companies like Chanel have used the number plate N0 5 on a delivery vehicle in London for decades. 車牌號碼向來都是重要的宣傳工具。某些機構，例如香奈爾，在過去數十年間一直利用車牌號碼是 N0 5 的送貨車在倫敦地區行走。

2) 信用卡號碼

信用卡號碼是一組複合標識符號，由 16 個數字組成，當中包含發卡機構、賬號、校驗等資料。

信用卡號碼的 16 個數字一般分成四組來閱讀或書寫，以方便溝通和理解。

比較以下兩種書寫方式：

- Easy:　　4036　3781　6643　9520
  Hard:　　4036378166439520

閱讀信用卡號碼時，可分四個數字為一組按節奏讀出，當中的空位
（space）無需刻意讀出。

- 4036　3781　6643　9520
  four O three six / three seven eight one / double six four three /
  nine five two O

※ 注意：其他如銀行賬戶號碼等大的數字，可以自行分組（如兩或三
個數字為一組）按節奏讀出。

學業成績

老師給學生的分數或成績叫 mark，美式英語叫 grade。學業成績一般以百份數來表示精確的分數。

- The highest mark was 92%. 最高分是 92 分。
- The pass mark is 60%. 及格分數是 60 分。
- He got 75 marks out of 100 for Putonghua. 他的普通話得了 75 分。

或以等級來表示成績的優劣高低。

- The highest mark was an A-. 最高分是 A-。
- The pass mark is a D. 及格分數是 D。
- She got a grade A in English. 她英語得了個 A。

mark（或 grade）可與 good / poor 或 high / low 搭配以表示成績。

- He got a good / poor mark in Maths. 他的數學成績是良 / 劣。
- His marks have been a lot lower this term. 他這學期的成績差多了。
- He always gets good marks. 他成績一直很好。

滿分是 full marks 或 top marks。

- She got full marks in Geography. 她地理拿滿分。

體育運動比賽結果

不同的體育運動有不同的計分方式和表達方法。

 籃球比賽

- Our team was leading (by) thirty (points) to twenty-seven at half time.
  我隊上半場以 30(分)比 27(分)領先。
- We gave away too many penalties in the second half.
  下半場犯規被罰球失分過多。
- Our opponents won sixty-two fifty-five.
  我們的對手以 62 對 55 獲勝。

羽毛球比賽

- He won the first game 21–16, lost the second 13–21 before both players were engaged in a gruelling third and deciding set.
  他以 21 比 16 贏了第一局，以 13 比 21 輸了第二局，兩名球員最後進入第三局的苦戰，也是決勝負的一局。

兵兵球比賽

- Wang Hao of China won the first set eleven eight (11–8).
  中國選手王皓以 11 比 8 贏了第一盤(局)。
- He dropped the second set eleven thirteen (11–13).
  他第二局以 11 比 13 的比分輸掉一局。
- He won the deciding set eleven nine (11–9).
  決定性的一局他以 11 比 9 獲勝。

足球比賽

- In the second half South China scored twice to equalize (3–3).
  在下半場比賽中，南華兩次射門得分，把比分扳平(3：3)。
- Five minutes from time, Kwok Kinpong scored from a penalty to give South China a four three victory. 完場前五分鐘，郭建邦罰球得分，結果南華以四比三(4：3)獲勝。
- Kitchee, at home to Macau, were held to a goalless draw/drew nil nil (0–0). 傑志對在主方場賽與澳門隊比賽，以零比零(0：0)踢成平局。

網球比賽

- After 39 minutes of battle, Li Na won the first set 6–4. 經過 39 分鐘的爭奪，李娜以 6–4 先下一盤
- In the second set, there was a transformation in the mentality of the lagging-behind Schiavone, but Li Na succeeded in blocking her, reaching the score of 2–0. 第二盤，比分落後的斯齊亞沃尼心態出現波動，李娜成功攔截她，後比分來到 2–0。
- In the tie-break, Li Na pressed on to finish. Schiavone lacked any capacity to fight back. Li Na obtained 6th championship points, ultimately successfully winning the match.
  在關鍵的搶七中李娜一鼓作氣，斯齊亞沃尼毫無還手之力。李娜一下子拿下了六個冠軍點，最終順利贏了比賽。

游泳

- He swam for his school in the men's 100 m（hundred metres）breaststroke.
  他代表學校參加男子 100 米蛙泳。
- She came first in the women's 400 m (four hundred metres) backstroke.
  她在女子 200 米仰泳（背泳）比賽中獲得第一名。
- Sun Yang broke the world record in the men's 1,500 m freestyle at the 2011 World Swimming Championships.
  孫楊在 2011 年的世界游泳錦標賽中打破了男子 1,500 米自由泳的世界紀錄。
- Michael Phelps won another Olympic gold medal in the men's 200 m individual medley at the London Olympic Games.
  菲爾普斯在男子 200 米個人混合泳比賽中奪得了他在倫敦奧運會上的另一枚金牌。

田徑

- She holds the school record for the women's 200 m (two hundred metres) hurdles.
  她保持 200 米女子跨欄的學校紀錄。
- He ran for his House in the men's 1500 m (fifteen hundred metres).
  他代表自己的學校分社參加男子千五米（賽跑）。
- I will run the men's 4 x 100 m (four by one hundred metres) relay on Sports Day.
  我會參加運動會的男子 4 x 100 米接力賽跑。

- She won a silver medal in the high jump, clearing a height of two metres. 她越過兩米的高度而贏得跳高銀牌。
- Mike Powell of the United States set the long jump world record 8.95 m (29.4 ft) during the 1991 World Championships held in Tokyo. 男子跳遠世界紀錄是美國運動員鮑威爾在 1991 年於東京舉行的世界錦標賽中創造的 8.95 米 (29.4 英尺) 佳績。
- The winner runner completed the course in 2 mins 13 secs. 比賽優勝者用 2 分 13 秒跑完全程。

※ 注意，我們一般把 0 唸成 zero。但在日常說話時，英國人也許會用 nought、O (讀作 oh) 或 nil。而 nil 一詞則多用來讀出比賽的記分。

- Our team won by three goals to nil. 我們隊以三比零獲勝。
- The teams drew nil-nil. 這兩隊以零比零打成平局。
- The score stood at one-nil with a minute left in the game. 比賽離完場還有一分鐘時，雙方的比分為一比零。

美國人在以上所有場合都會使用 zero。

骰子遊戲

一顆骰子有六面（faces），一般以基數詞 one 至 six 讀出，但要注意在專業的賭博遊戲中會用 ace、deuce、trey、cater、cinque 和 sice 來分別讀出骰子的六面。

擲骰的動作叫 roll。

 • The chance of rolling a six is always ⅙. 擲出 6 的機會永遠是六比一。

擲骰的數字總和叫 score。

 • The least possible total score must be 1 + 1 + 1 = 3. 擲骰的最小開數必定是 1 + 1 + 1 = 3。

六合彩

六合彩（Mark Six Lottery）是香港唯一的合法彩票，獲香港政府准許合法進行的賭博之一。

六合彩攪珠號碼分別用上基數和序數來表示。

- In each draw, seven numbers will be drawn out of 49 numbers. 每次抽獎時，均從 49 個數字彩球中抽出 7 個號碼。
- The first six numbers are the Drawn Numbers and the 7th number is the Extra Number. 首六個號碼為中獎號碼，第七個號碼為特別號碼。
- The second drawn number is twenty-eight. 第二個中獎號碼是二十八號。

7.2 速查表
Speed check

號碼的説法

一般號碼（如電話號碼）以基數詞讀出。

2626 2626	two six two six two six two six

如號碼中有重複數字，則用 double 表示。

2266 2266	double two double six double two double six

如號碼中有重複 3 次的數字，則用 triple 表示。

6222 6662	six triple two triple six two

08 AGE 年齡

日常對話中，少不免會談及年齡。How old are you / is your sister? 是詢問年齡最常見的問題。本節講述年齡的各種表達方式，除了人之外，還談及其他動植物的年歲。

8.1 怎樣用
Usage

 A 提及實際年齡

1) 提及自己或對方的實際年齡時，可以只用英語基數來交代年歲。用法是在 be 之後加上歲數。

- The baby is one. 寶寶一歲。
- I am sixteen. 我十六歲。
- Both of them are eighteen. 他們兩個都是十八歲。
- My grandmother is one hundred and one. 我外婆一百零一歲。

2) 想要強調的話，可在歲數後加上 years old。

- The baby is only one year old. 寶寶只有一歲大。
- I am sixteen years old. 我十六歲。
- Both of them are eighteen years old. 他們兩個都是十八歲。

3) 在正式的場合，尤其在書面語中，可在歲數後加上 years of age。

- One of the beauty pageant contestants is only thirteen years of age. 其中一名候選佳麗芳齡只得十三歲。
- One would guess him to be seventy years of age. 人們會以為他有七十歲了。

4) 如果年齡少於一歲的，就要清楚說明時間單位。

- a three-week-old fetus 三週大的胚胎
- a six-month-old baby 半歲大的寶寶

B 提及實際年齡的其他表達法

1) 在代表對方的名詞後加上 of，再加上歲數。

例
- a young woman of eighteen 芳齡十八的年輕女子
- an old man of sixty 花甲老翁
- When a man of forty falls in love with a girl of twenty, it isn't her youth he is seeking but his own.(Lenore J. Coffee)
  男人四十，愛上雙十年華的少女，與其說他在追求青春少艾，倒不如說他在找回自己失去的青春。

※ 注意，以上例子的 of 不能由 about 來替代。我們不能說 an old man about sixty，只能說 an old man of about sixty。

2) 在代表對方的名詞後加上 aged，再加上歲數。

例
- a woman aged forty 女人四十
- two young men aged nineteen and twenty-one 兩個年齡分別是 19 和 21 歲的年輕男士
- The course is designed for children aged 6 or above. 這課程針對六歲或以上的兒童而設計。
- The police are looking for a woman aged between 40 and 45. 警方正在通緝一名年約 40 至 45 歲的女人。

3) 用數字構成的複合形容詞（compound adjective）來表示，後接代表
對方的名詞。

- a three-month-old baby 三個月大的寶寶
- a twenty-year-old undergraduate 二十歲的本科生
- The news about Mary Bell, a 10-year-old English girl who killed several children, was too shocking! 十歲英國女童貝瑪莉殺死了數名兒童，簡直駭人聽聞！

※ 注意，作為放在名詞之前的形容詞，month 和 year 之後不加 s，以上例子並不能用 a three-months-old baby、a twenty-years-old undergraduate 來表達。

4) 用數字構成的複合名詞（compound noun）來表示。

- There is only one twelve-year-old in this class. 這班只有一個學生是十二歲。
- Why are two-year-olds so terrible? 為何兩歲大的都是這麼難管？

C　提及大概的年齡

1) 如不能準確說出某人年齡或不願說出真實年齡，一般會在表示年齡的數字前加上諸如 about、almost、nearly、under、over 等字眼。

- ladies over 65　六十五歲以上的女士
- people who are under 25　凡 25 歲以下者
- Mr Chan is almost forty. 陳先生差不多四十歲了。
- I think she's about fifty. 我猜她五十歲左右吧。
- Aunt Toto must be nearly sixty. 嘟嘟姨姨應該快六十歲了。

2) 比較正式的說法是 below / above the age of。

- No one below the age of 21 was involved in the making of this film. 此電影沒有 21 歲以下人士參與演出。
- How many citizens are above the age of 60? 年滿 60 的居民一共有多少？

3) 表示某十年之間的歲數，例如 20 至 29 歲之間是 in someone's twenties，30 至 39 歲之間是 in someone's thirties，如此類推。

- She's in her forties. 她四十多歲。
- Aunt Toto must be in her sixties. 嘟嘟姨姨應該六十多歲了。

※ 注意，上例可加 early、middle、late 以表達該十年間的前、中、後三個年齡階段，例如 in her early forties（四十開外）、in her late sixties（接近七十歲）等。

※ 注意，in his / her teens 特指 13 至 19 歲之間的青少年時代。

- She's in her teens when her family moved to Toronto. 她的家人移居到多倫多時她才十幾歲。

※ 注意，可加 early 和 late 以表達較前和較後的年齡階段，例如 in her early teens（她十三四歲時）、in his late teens（他十八九歲時）。

4) 在非正式說法中，表示某十年之間的歲數還可以用 twentysomething
或 thirtysomething 來表示。

- He's a thirtysomething. 他三十幾歲。
- A large crowd of twentysomethings were gathered before the Central Government offices. 一大群二十來歲的人聚集在政府總部外面。

⊕ **中英文比較**

中文對年齡的稱謂很多都是來自古語，例如「繈褓」指 1 歲以下的嬰孩，「孩提」是 2 至 3 歲的幼童，「豆蔻年華」指約 13 至 16 歲的少年時代，「志學之年」是 15 歲的少年，「二八年華」指十五六歲最美好的青春時代，「加冠之年」指 20 歲，「而立之年」指 30 歲，「不惑之年」為 40 歲，「知命之年」為 50 歲，「耳順、還曆、花甲之年」均指 60 歲，「從心或古稀之年」即是 70 歲，「耄耋之年」就是八九十歲，而「期頤之年」則指百歲之高壽，又稱作「人瑞」。

提及事物的年齡

1) 除了人之外，動物當然也可用歲數計算年齡。

- her ten-day-old puppies 她那些十天大的小狗
- A two-week-old kitten needs to be bottle fed. 兩週大的小貓需要用奶樽來餵養。

2) 建築物、汽車等也不例外。

- his five-year-old Honda Civic 他那輛開了五年的本田思域轎車
- fossils 30 million years old 三千萬年前的化石
- The church is about a hundred years old. 這座教堂約有100年。

※ 注意，與表示人物的年齡不同，我們不能只用英語基數來交代死物年歲。

比較：

✓ Grandpa's about one hundred.
✗ The church is about one hundred.

3) 提及事物的年齡，還有別的表達方式。

- Tang bronze mirrors 唐代銅鏡
- a Victorian building 維多利亞時代的建築物
- a medieval castle 中世紀時代的城堡
- an eighth-century theatre 八世紀的劇院
- life in fifth-century Athens 五世紀的雅典生活
- 'How old's the church?' 'I think it was built about 1900 / more than a hundred years ago.' "這教堂有多長歷史？" "我想它是在 1900 年左右興建的 / 一百多年前建造的。"

8.2 速查表
Speed check

年齡的不同說法

✓ John is twenty something.

✓ John is a twentysomething.

✓ John is twenty-four.

✓ John Chen is twenty-four years old.

✓ John Chen is twenty-four years of age.

✓ John Chen is over twenty-one.

✓ John Chen is almost twenty-five.

✓ John Chen is under twenty-five.

✓ John Chen is in his (middle) twenties.

✓ John Chen is a young man of twenty-four.

✓ John Chen, aged 24, is a teacher.

✓ John Chen, a 24-year-old teacher, won the Marathon.

09 TIME 時間

時間一般以基數來表示。

9.1 怎樣用
Usage

A 時間單位

測量時間所用的基本單位,從小到大排列如下。

時間單位

1 second 秒 *	
1 minute 分鐘	= 60 seconds
1 quarter 刻	= 15 minutes
1 hour 小時	= 60 minutes
1 day 日	= 24 hours
1 week 星期	= 7 days
1 fortnight 兩週	= 2 weeks or 14 days
1 month 月	= 28 to 31 days, or about 4 weeks
1 season 季	= 3 months
1 year 年	= 52 weeks, or 12 months, or 365 days
1 decade 年代;十年期	= 10 years
1 century 世紀	= 100 years
1 millennium 千年	= 10 centuries or 1000 years

* 秒可進一步細分為飛秒、皮秒、納秒、微秒,但這不在本書討論範圍。

B 如何表達時間

1) 正點時間用 o'clock 表示。

- two o'clock 兩點正
- 'What time did you get back to Hong Kong?''Nine o'clock.'
  "你甚麼時候回到香港？""九點鐘。"

※ 注意，用 o'clock 報時必須以文字而不是阿拉伯數字來書寫，譬如 two o'clock 不能寫成 2 o'clock；此外，o'clock 中的 o 要唸成輕聲的 /ə/，而不是英語字母 O 的發音 /oʊ/。

2) 有時表示正點時間時 o'clock 甚至可以刪掉。

- I usually get up at eight in the morning. 我早上通常八點起來。
- Come around at five. 五點鐘過來吧。
- I'll be back at ten. 我十點鐘回來。
- I work until nine. 我一直工作到九點。

3) 正點之後的十五和三十分鐘（即時間是十五和三十分時），分別用 a quarter past 和 half past 來表示。

- a quarter past three 三點一刻（三點十五分）
- 'What time do they open?''Half past ten.' "他們幾點鐘開門？""十點半。"

※ 注意，這種說法不能加上 o'clock，例如不能說 half past ten o'clock。

4) 至於四十五分時（意指下一個正點之前的十五分鐘）用 a quarter to
來報時。

- a quarter to five 四點三刻（四點四十五分）
- 'What's the time now?' 'A quarter to eight.'
  "現在幾點鐘？" "七點四十五分。"

※ 注意，這種說法不能加上 o'clock，例如不能說 a quarter to five o'clock。

5) 小時內的其餘分鐘都可以用 to 或 past 來表示。

- It's five to six. 五點五十五分。
- We got to the airport at twenty past two. 我們在兩點二十分到
  達機場。

※ 注意，這種說法一般不加上 minutes，例如不說 twenty minutes past
two。除非要強調極為準確的某分鐘則屬例外。

- The bomb exploded at twelve minutes to twelve. 炸彈在 11 時
  48 分爆炸。

6) 可加上介詞短語表示一天內的某時段。

- It's four o'clock in the afternoon. 現在是下午四點鐘。
- They worked from nine thirty in the morning until eight thirty
  at night. 他們從早上九點半開始一直工作到晚上八點半為止。
- The party began at seven in the evening. 派對在晚上七點開始。

7) 在美語中，常以 after 替代 past，以 of 替代 to。

- It's five of six. 五點五十五分。
- We got to the airport at twenty after two. 我們在兩點二十分到達機場。

8) 在口語中，如果雙方已意會時間所指，則無須說出特定那個小時。

- 'What time is it?' 'It's a quarter past.'
  "現在幾點鐘？" "十五分。"

9) 時間可以直接用作修飾語。

- They got in the three o'clock high speed rail to Wuhan.
  他們乘坐了三點鐘的高鐵前往武漢。
- I usually watch the eight o'clock news before dinner.
  我通常在晚飯前收看八點新聞報導。

⊕ 中英文比較

中國傳統的報時中有「時辰」和「旬」之說，這是英語世界裏沒有的時間單位。一個時辰等於兩個小時，一天共十二個時辰，例如：半個時辰前，他陪伴天子酣宴。（曹禺《王昭君》）「時辰」也可泛指時間，例如：這等幹，只是忒費事，耽擱了時辰了。（吳承恩《西遊記》第四十九回）。而一旬等於十天，一月分為上、中、下三旬，例如：此時是六月下旬天氣，帶行李的甚少。（吳趼人《二十年目睹之怪現象》）

使用國際時間

1) 其實無論是否正點、十五分、三十分或是四十五分，我們只需用 1 至 59 的基數詞讀法，就可表達所有時間，尤其是使用國際時間的時候。

- 1.59   one fifty-nine
- 6.30   six thirty
- 12.00   twelve
- 23.45   twenty-three forty-five

時與分之間用點號（.），但注意一些美國人會用冒號（:）代替點號。

2) 用 a.m. 來表示深夜 12 點到正午 12 點的時段；用 p.m. 來表示正午 12 點至深夜 12 點的時段。

- They woke up at 3 a.m. 他們在凌晨三點鐘就起牀了。
- The plane arrived at 11.30 p.m. 航班於晚上十一點半抵達。

※ 注意，a.m. / p.m. 也可寫作 am. / pm.、A.M. / P.M. 或 AM / PM。

※ 注意，a.m. 和 p.m. 不用於口語中；也不能與 o'clock 同用，譬如不說 3 o'clock a.m.。

3) 書寫時間時，中午和午夜一般不寫成 12 p.m. 和 12 a.m.，而是用 noon 和 midnight 來表達。

- We got there around midnight and slept until noon the next day. 我們到達時已是深夜，然後一睡就睡到第二天中午。

4) 這種報時方式也可以直接用作修飾語。

- We were able to catch the seven thirty (train) to Guangzhou. 我們趕上了七點半出發前往廣州的列車。
- He goes to bed right after the 11 p.m. news every night. 他每晚看完十一點新聞報導後便睡覺。

不具體標示時間

1) 如不能準確說出時間，一般會在時間之前加上 about、around、just before、just after 等字眼。

- We left about seven o'clock. 我們大約七點離開了。
- The show will begin at around eight. 演出大概在八點鐘開始。
- Shortly after five when I was about to leave, my boss called a meeting. 剛過了五點，我準備離開時，老闆就召開會議。
- She has come home just before twelve o'clock. 她剛在十二點前回到家裏。

有時會在鐘點後加上 -ish 以表示大概的時間。

- Shall I come over about sevenish? 我可以七點左右過來嗎？
- Ring me at eightish. 八點左右給我打電話吧。

2) 但更多時候會看到以下其他說法。

- 'When did you come?' 'Just after dinner.' "你甚麼時候來的？" "剛吃完飯就來了。"
- See you in the afternoon. 下午見。
- We are going to fly to Okinawa tomorrow morning. 我們明天早上出發飛往沖繩島。
- At sunset we will visit the Okinawa Churaumi Aquarium. 黃昏時份我們會去遊覽沖繩美麗海水族館。

其他指日出日落時份的短語包括：at dawn, at first light, at dusk, at sunset, at daybreak, at sunrise, at nightfall, at twilight。

9.2 速查表
Speed check

時間的讀法

表示上午的時間：使用 a.m. 或 in the morning。
9 a.m. / nine o'clock in the morning 上午 9 時
10:25 a.m. / twenty-five past ten in the morning 上午 10 時 25 分

表示下午的時間：使用 p.m. 或 in the afternoon / in the evening / at night。
3 p.m. / three o'clock in the afternoon 下午 3 時
6:30 p.m. / half past six in the evening 下午 6 時 30 分
9:45 p.m. / a quarter to ten at night 晚上 9 時 45 分

10 DAYS AND DATES 日期

10.1 怎樣用
Usage

A | **兩種表示日期的方式**

1) 在英語中,有兩種表示日期的方式,一是先說月份,一是先說日子,例如 1 月 1 日,便可以說成 January the first 或 the first of January。

   例 • A: When is your birthday?
   • B: My birthday is on January the first. **OR**
      My birthday is on the first of January.

   ※ 注意,很多時候,前置詞 on 甚至可以刪去:
   • My birthday is January the first.
   • My birthday is the first of January.

2) 以上這些說法在英國和澳洲兩地普遍採用。美國人多以月份開始,而且把 the 刪去,說法比較簡單俐落。

   例 • A: When is your birthday?
      B: My birthday is January first.
   • A: What day were you born on?
      B: I was born on April third.
   • A: What's the date?
      B: It's June seventh.

B 年份的説法

年份通常用阿拉伯數字表示,用基數詞讀出。

1) 英語中一般把年份分成兩半來說就萬無一失。

例
- 989 > 9 89 = nine eighty-nine
- 1911 > 19 11 = nineteen eleven
- 1949 > 19 49 = nineteen forty-nine
- 1997 > 19 97 = nineteen ninety-seven
- 2010 > 20 10 = twenty ten

※ 注意,被問及出生年份(What year were you born in?)時可以回答 I was born in (the year) 1990. ,切勿長篇大論地把年份 1990 說成 one thousand nine hundred and ninety。

2) 如果後截數值少於十,有人會加上英語字母 O 的發音,即 /oʊ/。

例
- 1901 > 19 01   nineteen oh one

3) 假使年份以 00(即百年)終結,例如 1800、1900,把後半讀成 hundred 就行。

例
- 1800 > 18 00 = eighteen hundred
- 1900 > 19 00 = nineteen hundred

4) 假使年份以 000(即千禧年)終結,例如 1000、 2000 ,一般寫作 the year 1000 和 the year 2000 ,讀作 the year one thousand 和 the year two thousand。

5) 年代用年份的阿拉伯數字加 -'s 或 -s 表示。

例
- 1720's 或 1720s 十八世紀二十年代

初期、中期、末期分別用 early，mid- 和 late 表示。

- the early thirties　三十年代初期
- the mid-thirties　三十年代中期
- the late thirties　三十年代末期
- the early 1960's　二十世紀六十年代初期
- the mid-1960's　二十世紀六十年代中期
- the late 1960's　二十世紀六十年末期

6) 公元前用 BC（= Before Christ；美式英語：B.C.）表示，公元用 AD（= Anno Domini（i.e. in the year of our lord）；美式英語：A.D.）表示，讀其字母音。

- 502 BC（讀：five hundred and two BC）公元前 502 年
- 429 AD（讀：AD four hundred and twenty-nine）公元 429 年
- Alexander the Great was born in 356 BC. 阿歷山大帝生於公元前 356 年。
- The Great Pyramid dates from around 2600 BC. 大金字塔建於公元前 2600 年左右。
- Confucius was born in 551 BC in the Lu state of China. 公元前 551 年，孔子生於中國魯國。

※ 注意，AD 一般用於公元 1 年到公元 999 年之間的年份。公元 1000 年以後的年份不用刻意標識。

- 65 AD　　　　　　　　公元 65 年
- the first century AD　公元一世紀
- 1997　　　　　　　　（公元）1997 年
- Queen Elizabeth I 1558–1603（讀：Queen Elizabeth the First reigned from fifteen fifty-eight to sixteen O three）
  伊利莎伯女王一世從 1558 年到 1603 年在位

✛ 中英文比較

干支曆作為中國傳統曆法，一直沿用至今。干支是天干與
地支的合稱，由兩者經一定的組合方式搭配，用以記錄干支
紀年、農曆月日、歷史朝代紀年、生肖屬相以及其他傳統
上採用漢字形式的非西曆紀年等，但換作英語時無需刻意
譯出，否則外國人看不明白，例如：

- 八月十五中秋 Mid-Autumn Festival
- 甲午戰爭（=1894 年）First Sino-Japanese War
- 戊戌維新（=1898 年）Hundred Days Reform
- 辛亥革命（=1911 年）Chinese Revolution of 1911
- 清光緒三十年（=1904 年）
  the 30th year of the Guangxu reign (1904)
- 永和九年，歲在癸丑（= 公元 353 年），暮春之初，會於會
  稽山陰之蘭亭。（王羲之《蘭亭序》）In early March of year
  353, the ninth year of the Yonghe reign, we gathered at Orchid
  Pavilion in the north of Mount Guiji.
- 據說丙猴年出生的人充滿好奇心。People born in the year of
  the monkey are said to be full of curiosity.
- 香港郵政今日發行新一套農曆新年 "歲次乙未（羊年）"
  特別郵票。A set of new CNY special stamps for the 'Year of
  the Ram' was issued by Hongkong Post today.

年月日的書寫次序

1) 日期（包括年、月、日）的書寫方式也不盡相同。在英式英語中，一般的次序是日、月、年。

- 1 January 1988
- 3 June 1997
- 10 September 2015

日子可用序數來書寫，即加上 -st、-nd、-rd、-th 等。

- 1st January 1988
- 3rd June 1997
- 10th September 2015

2) 如果日期出現在句子中，月與年之間必須加上逗號。

- I was born on 1st January, 1988.

3) 注意在讀出日期時，通常要加上 the 和 of。例如，31st December, 2012 會讀成 (the) thirty-first of December two thousand and twelve。

4) 在美式英語中，一般以月份開始，次序是月日年，日與年之間必須加上逗號。

- January 1, 1988
- June 3, 1997
- September 10, 2015

5) 在英式及美式英語中，月份都可用縮寫來表示。

- （英）1 Jan 1988
- （美）Jan 1, 1998

6) 只用數字來表達年、月、日時,英式英語的次序是日、月、年,美式英語則是月、日、年

 • (英) 25.12.2013
• (美) 12.25.2013

※ 注意,同樣的幾個數字,例如 1.7.1997,對於英國人來說,是代表 1997 年 7 月 1 日,可是對於美國人來說,卻是 1997 年 1 月 7 日!

7) 此外,除了用點號(.)來間隔年月日,也可用連字符號(-)或斜線號(/)來代替點號。

 • (英) 1.9.1997   1-9-1997   1/9/1997
• (美) 9.1.1997   9-1-1997   9/1/1997

⊕ 中英文比較

英文日期的書寫次序以年份為末,中文則以年份為始。中文的書寫次序是年、月、日(如:1997 年 7 月 1 日),與英式英語的日、月、年或美式英語的月、日、年不同。

10.2 速查表
Speed check

日期的寫法和讀法

	英式英語	美式英語
日期的寫法	一般的次序是日、月、年 1 July 2015 或 1st July 2015 1 Jul. 2015 或 1st Jul. 2015 1-7-2015 或 1-7-15 1/7/2015 1/7/15	一般的次序是月、日、年 July 1, 2015 或 July 1st, 2015 Jul. 1, 2015 或 Jul. 1st, 2015 8-1-2015 或 7-1-15 7/1/2015 7/1/15
日、月的讀法	先說日、後說月。例如 10 月 1 日讀作 the first of October。	先說月、後說日。例如 10 月 1 日讀作 October the first。
年份的讀法	在英語中，一般把年份分成兩半來說，英式英語和美式英語沒有差別，例如： 1949 年 分成 19 和 49 兩半，讀作 nineteen forty-nine 1997 年 分成 19 和 97 兩半，讀作 nineteen ninety-seven 2015 年 分成 20 和 15 兩半，讀作 twenty fifteen 2000 年則直接說成 the year two thousand。	

MONEY AND CHEQUES 貨幣與支票

貨幣是用作交易媒介、儲藏價值和記賬的一種工具,既包括流通貨幣(即實際應用的紙幣或硬幣),也包括各種儲蓄存款。

11.1 怎樣用
Usage

 英美地區

1) 美金

美國的官方貨幣是美金(United States Dollar),又叫美圓、美元,代號 USD*;貨幣符號為 US$ 。

如果以數字表達貨幣幣值,用符號 $ 或 USD ,後接金額,例如美金 100 元可寫成 US$100 ,讀作 one hundred US dollars 。

2) 英鎊

英國國家貨幣是英鎊(Pound Sterling)* ,又叫新英鎊(New Pound),代號 GBP(Great Britain Pound);貨幣符號為 £ 。英國的基本貨幣單位是英鎊(pounds)和便士(pence)。一英鎊等於 100 便士。

如果以數字表達貨幣幣值,用符號 £ 或 GBP ,後接金額,例如 100 英鎊可寫成 £100 ,讀作 one hundred pounds 。

* 指國際標準化組織的ISO 4217國際標準貨幣代碼,每種貨幣以常用的三位字母代表。
** 英國雖然是歐盟的成員國,但尚未加入歐元區,故仍然使用英鎊。

中港台澳地區

由於歷史因素，中華人民共和國有三種不同的法定貨幣，大陸地區使用人民幣，港澳地區因為實行一國兩制，香港法定貨幣是港元，澳門則是澳門元。而中華民國台澎金馬地區使用新臺幣。

1) 人民幣

大陸地區使用人民幣 (China Yuan)，代號 CNY，簡寫 RMB (Renminbi)；貨幣符號為 ￥，讀音為 yuan。人民幣的單位為元，人民幣輔幣單位為角、分，口語常以塊代元、毛代角。主輔幣換算關係：1 元等於 10 角。

如果以數字表達貨幣幣值，用符號 ￥ 或 RMB￥（以區別於日元），後接金額，例如人民幣 100 元可寫成 ￥100 或 RMB￥100，讀作 one hundred yuan。

2) **港元**

HK$

香港特別行政區的法定貨幣是港元 (Hong Kong Dollars)，又叫港幣，代號 HKD，貨幣符號為 HK$。港幣的單位為「圓」，簡稱「元」，口語常以蚊代圓、毫代角。

如果以數字表達貨幣幣值，用符號 HK$，後接金額，例如一百港元可寫成 HK$100，讀作 one hundred Hong Kong Dollars。

3) 新台幣

NT$

中華民國臺澎金馬地區使用新台幣（Taiwan Dollars），代號是 TWD，貨幣符號為 NT$、NTD。其基本單位為「圓」，簡稱「元」，口語常以塊代圓、毛代角。

如果以數字表達貨幣幣值，用符號 NT$，後接金額，例如一百新臺幣可寫成 NT$100，讀作 one hundred Taiwan dollars。

4) 澳元

MOP$

澳門法定貨幣是澳門幣（Macau Pataca），俗稱葡幣，代號 MOP，貨幣符號為 MOP$、pts。其基本單位為「圓」，簡稱「元」，口語常以蚊代圓、毫代角。主輔幣換算關係為 1 Pataca = 100 Avos（1 元等於 100 仙）。

如果以數字表達貨幣幣值，用符號 MOP$，後接金額，例如澳門幣可寫成 MOP$100，正式讀作 one hundred Macanese patacas。但由於澳門受香港影響，以英語表達澳門幣銀碼時，都習慣用港元的英語說法，即是把澳門幣稱為 Macau dollar 而不說 Macanese pataca，或把 $20.5 說成 twenty dollars and fifty cents 而不說 twenty patacas and fifty avos。

價錢的讀法

1) 一般來說，價錢以閱讀基數詞的方法讀出便可。

- $150   a hundred and fifty dollars 一百五十元
- $1,362   one thousand, three hundred and sixty-two dollars 一千三百六十二元
- $2,275   two thousand, two hundred and seventy-five dollars 二千二百七十五元
- $10,000   ten thousand dollars 一萬元
- $150,000   one hundred, fifty thousand dollars 十五萬元
- $3,000,000 three million dollars 三百萬元

2) cent 以符號 c 表示。

- 50 c   （不能讀作 fifty c）
  fifty cents   五角

如數額包括 dollar 和 cent，則 c 不用標示。

- $138.20   （不能寫作 $138.20 c）
  one hundred and thirty-eight dollars twenty cents
  一百三十八元二角

在口語中，dollars 和 cents 甚至不會讀出。

- 'How much is that?' 'Eight dollars sixty.'
  "多少錢？" "八塊六。"
- All right then, fine, that's thirty-three fifty then, please.
  好的，那麼，就是三十三塊五毛，謝謝。

3) 為了簡潔起見，金額巨大的貨幣有時會以略語表示，即以 k 代 thousand、以 m 代 million、以 bn 代 billion。

- $1.6 m 一百六十萬元
- an annual salary of US$150K + bonus 年薪十五萬美元外加獎金
- junior staff earning less than $100K per annum 年收入少於十萬元的低級職員
- a massive investment of $30bn to rebuild economy 三百億元的大量投資以振興經濟

4) 紙幣和硬幣分別以 note 和 coin 表示。

- Can you give me change for a twenty-dollar note?
  可以給我換二十元紙幣的零錢嗎？
- You didn't have a fifty-dollar note, did you?
  你沒有五十元的紙幣，是不是？
- The machine wouldn't take 2-dollar coins.
  這台機器不收兩元硬幣。

5) 與 cost 或 worth of 等詞語搭配以表達貨品價值。

- a powerful smartphone costing over six thousand dollars
  價格高於六千元的功能強大的智慧型電話
- It would cost me around two thousand. 我要花上大概兩千元。
- He owns some three billion dollars worth of property in Beijing.
  他在北京擁有的物業價值三億元左右。
- 'How much does this painting cost?' 'It costs $100,000.'
  "這幅畫要多少錢？""十萬元。"

填寫支票

銀行、單位和個人填寫的各種票據、支票和結算憑證是辦理支付結算和現金收付的重要依據；因此，填寫時必須做到數字正確、字跡清晰、不錯漏、不潦草。

1) 寫英文支票必須以全寫大楷或各單字首字為大楷寫出，但注意 and 要用小楷。

• $4,242.42
Four Thousand Two Hundred (and) Forty-two Dollars and
Forty-two Cents Only
• $56,202.02
Fifty-six Thousand Two Hundred (and) Two Dollars and
Two Cents Only

※ 注意：Hundred 與 Dollars 之間是可以加 and，這是英式與美式英語之別，兩者皆可。

2) 如支票上已印有諸如 Hong Kong Dollars 等字樣，則無需寫上 Dollars 亦可。如不書寫 Dollars，則 Cents 必須寫在數字前面，以求統一。

• $11,245.63
Eleven Thousand Two Hundred Forty Five and Cents
Sixty Three Only

3) 表示一百、一千、一百萬等時需明確寫出 one，而不能用不定代詞 a 替代。

• $101,100
One Hundred Thousand, One Thousand and
One Hundred Only
(Not A Hundred Thousand, A Hundred and A Hundred Only)

✪ 中英文比較

中文大寫數字多用於發票、匯款、財務等金額總計中，此等金額數字應用正楷或行書填寫，如：壹、貳、叁、肆、伍、陸、柒、捌、玖、拾、佰、仟、萬、億、元、角、分、零、整（正）等字樣，不得用一、二（兩）、三、四、五、六、七、八、九、十、毛、或0填寫。中文大寫金額數字到「元（圓）」為止，在「元」之後寫「正（整）」字；在「角」或「分」之後無需重複「正（整）」字，例如金額 $11,245.63 必須寫成「壹萬壹仟貳佰肆拾伍圓正陸角三分」。

11.2 速查表
Speed check

金錢的讀法

$0.01	One cent	一分
$0.1	Ten cents	一角
$0.5	Fifty cents	五角
$0.75	Seventy-five cents	七分五角
$1	One dollar	一元
$7.6	Seven dollars and sixty cents	七元六角
$10	Ten dollars	十元
$39	Thirty-nine dollars	三十九元
$84.7	Eighty-four dollars and seventy cents	八十四元七角
$100	One hundred dollars	一百元
$562.5	Five hundred and sixty-two dollars and fifty cents	五百六十二元 五角
$1,000	One thousand dollars	一千元
$3,969	Three thousand, nine hundred and sixty-nine dollars	三千九百六十九元
$10,000	Ten thousand dollars	一萬元
$45,000	Forty-five thousand dollars	四萬五千元
$150,000	One hundred and fifty thousand dollars	十五萬元
$663,550.31	Six hundred and sixty-three thousand, five hundred and fifty dollars and thirty-one cents	六十六萬 三千五百五十元 三角一分
$1,000,000	One million dollars	一百萬元
$3,998,000	Three million, nine hundred and ninety-eight thousand dollars	三百九十九萬 八千元
$99,000,000	Ninety-nine million dollars	九千九百萬元

12 MEASUREMENTS 計量

計量就是測定物體的尺吋（如長度、寬度、高度、面積、容量、速度及溫度等）。

12.1 怎樣用
Usage

A 公制與英制

關於計量問題，首先要掌握如何利用計量單位。

公制（或稱米制）（Metric system）是一個國際化的十進制量度系統，已成為世界上大多數國家的主要量度系統。英制（British system）單位則是一種源自英國的度量衡單位制。

十進制的公制單位使用方便，多為各國採行，但由於傳統和習慣使然，國際上許多個別領域仍沿用英制；例如電視機、電腦顯示屏、手機熒幕大小多以英吋表示；陸路交通仍以英哩作為單位；航空管制上，如飛行高度、跑度長度等，也多以英呎為單位。

以下說明同時列出公制與英制的計量單位。

B 長度 (Length)

1) 在表達長 (length)、寬 (width)、高 (height)、距離 (distance) 等時，在日常生活中，最常用的長度單位是 cm (厘米)、m (米；公尺)、km (千米；公里)。

公制長度單位			
1 millimetre (mm) 毫米			
1 centimetre (cm) 厘米	= 10 mm		
1 decimetre (dm) 分米	= 10 cm	= 100 mm	
1 metre (m) 米；公尺	= 10 dm	= 100 cm	= 1,000 mm
1 decametre (dam) 十米	= 10 m	= 100 dm	= 1,000 cm
1 hectometre (hm) 百米	= 10 dam	= 100 m	= 1,000 dm
1 kilometre (km) 千米；公里	= 10 hm	= 100 dam	= 1,000 m

- a 180 cm bed 一張 180 厘米長的牀
- A standard A4 size paper measures 210 mm wide and 297 mm long. 標準的 A4 紙張長 297 mm、闊 210 mm。
- The Titanic was about 260 metres in length. 鐵達尼號的船身長約 260 米。
- The Tsing Ma Bridge is 2.2 km long. 青馬大橋總長 2.2 公里。

2) 在英制的長度名稱中，為了與公制或中國傳統單位區別，多在單位前加一個「英」字，或冠以口字旁稱之，如：英里（英哩）、英尺（英呎）、英寸（英吋），或簡稱哩、呎、吋。

英制長度單位			
1 inch (in) 英寸；吋			
1 foot (ft) 英尺；呎	= 12 in		
1 yard (yd) 碼	= 36 in	= 3 feet	
1 mile (m) 英里	= 66,330 in	= 5,280 feet	= 31,760 yards

- He's about 5 feet 10 inches(tall). 他身高 5 英尺 10 英寸。
- Mount Parker is 1,745 ft high. 柏架山的高度為 1,745 英尺。
- She's 36-24-38 (i.e. the circumference of her bust, waist and hips is 36, 24 and 38 inches respectively). 她三圍是 36-24-38。
- He takes a 15.5 collar (i.e. his neck is 15.5 inches in circumference). 他領子的周長是 15.5 英寸。
- The box is 30 inches long, 15 inches wide and 8 inches deep. 這個箱子長 30 英寸、寬 15 英寸、高 8 英寸。
- Silk in this shop is sold by the yard. 這家商店的絲綢按碼出售。
- a 300-mile journey 三百英里的旅程

3) 表達距離時，各長度單位使用複數形式，並在其後加上 from、away from、apart 等字眼。

- 100 metres from the beach 距離海灘一百米以外
- about 10 kilometres away from downtown 與市中心相距大約 10 公里
- The two villages are five miles apart. 兩個村莊相隔 5 英里遠。

4) 談及圓形物體的尺寸時，用圓周或直徑來表示。用法是長度單位 + in circumference 或長度單位 + in diameter。

- It is five metres in circumference. 這東西的圓周是五米。
- They are about one foot in diameter. 它們的直徑大約有一尺。

重量 (Weight)

1) 在日常生活中，最常用的重量單位是 gram（克）和 kilogram（千克）。

公制重量單位			
1 milligram (mg) 毫克			
1 centigram (cg) 厘克	= 10 mg		
1 decigram (dg) 分克	= 10 cg	= 100 mg	
1 gram (g) 克	= 10 dg	= 100 cg	= 1,000 mg
1 decagram (dag) 十克	= 10 g	= 100 dg	= 1,000 cg
1 hectogram (hg) 百克	= 10 dag	= 100 g	= 1,000 dg
1 kilogram (kg) 千克；公斤	= 10 hg	= 100 dag	= 1,000 g
1 tonne 公噸			

1) 表達重量時，一般用動詞 weigh，並在其後加上 kg 等計量單位。

- How much does a parcel weighing 200 grams cost by mail from Hong Kong to Beijing? 兩百克的包裹，從香港寄去北京郵費要多少？
- The baby weighs 4.2 kg. 寶寶重 4.2 公斤。
- An average African elephant weighs 2.7 to 6 tonnes. 非洲象的體重介乎 2.7 至 6 公噸之間。

2) 英制中的常用重量單位是 ounce（盎司）和 pound（磅）。

英制重量單位	
1 ounce (oz) 盎司	
1 pound (lb) 磅	= 16 oz
1 stone 英石	= 14 lb
1 quarter 夸特	= 2 stones
1 hundredweight	= 100 lb
1 ton (ton) 噸	= 2,000 lb

- There are 16 ounces in a pound. 一磅有十六盎司。
- She has put on over ten pounds. 她的體重已增加了十多磅。
- A blue whale can eat some four to nine tons of krill per day.
  一條藍鯨每天可進食四至九噸磷蝦。

3) 英國人常用 stone（英石）作為體重的量度單位。一英石等於 14 磅或 6.35 公斤。

- He weighs thirteen and a half stone. 他的體重是 13.5 英石。
- I am nine stone four. 我的體重是九英石四磅。

※ 注意，stone 不作複數形式用。如 stone 後接磅數，則通常 pound 省略不同，譬如上例不說 nine stone four pounds。

4) 慣用語 weigh a ton 是個誇張的比喻，指「非常重」而已。

- That piano weighs a ton. You need three men to lift it. 他那座鋼琴重得不得了，要三人合力才能搬動。

5) 重量單位可作定語用，置於名詞前。

- a two-kilogram bag of pebbles 一包兩公斤的卵石
- a 20-stone man 重 20 英石的男人
- A 500-pound bomb was dropped on the island. 一個五百磅重的炸彈投擲到島上。

⊕ 中英文比較

在不少華人地區，例如香港，雖然已正式引入公制，但中國舊制仍被廣泛用於糧食（如海味和藥材方面的買賣）和貴金屬的買賣，當中以 1 擔 = 100 司馬斤、1 斤 = 16 兩、1 兩 = 10 錢、1 錢 = 10 分等換算。

D 面積 (Area)

1) 在日常生活中，最常用的面積單位是 square metre（平方米／平方公尺），簡稱 m^2。

公制面積單位		
1 square millimetre (mm^2) 平方毫米		
1 square centimetre (cm^2) 平方厘米	= 100 mm^2	
1 square metre (m^2) 平方米；平方公尺	= 100 cm^2	= 10,000 mm^2
1 acre 公畝	= 100 m^2	= 10,000 cm^2
1 hectare (ha) 公頃	= 100 acres	= 10,000 m^2
1 square kilometre (km^2) 平方公里	= 100 ha	= 10,000 acres

表達面積時，各長度單位使用複數形式，並在其前加上 square（平方）即可。

- 45 square metres 45 平方米
- a 10-hectare coal mine 一塊十公頃的煤礦
- It has an area of more than 100 square kilometres. 它的面積超過 100 平方公里。

2) 在英制中，常用的面積單位是 square foot（平方英尺）。

英制面積單位		
1 square inch 平方英寸		
1 square foot 平方英尺	= 144 平方英寸	
1 square yard 平方碼	= 9 平方英尺	
1 acre 英畝	= 4,840 平方碼	= 43,560 平方英尺
1 square mile 平方英里	= 640 英畝	= 3,097,600 平方碼

- The room is 86 square feet in area. 這個房間的面積是 86 平方英尺。
- What is the area of a football field in square yards? 足球場的面積是多少平方碼？
- a 15-acre country park near Sai Kung 靠近西貢的一塊 15 英畝的郊野公園
- They own 1.5 square miles of farmland in Guangzhou. 他們在廣州擁有 1.5 平方英里的農田。

⊕ 中英文比較

香港政府賣地一般使用國際單位 hectare（公頃）來計算土地面積，然而地產界方面卻偏好使用 square foot（每平方英尺）價格來比較樓宇價值。台灣則以「甲」(1 甲 = 9,699.173 m^2) 和「坪」(1 坪 = 3.3058 m^2) 來計算面積。

容量 (Capacity)

1) 在日常生活中，最常用的容量單位是 litre（公升／升），簡稱 l。

公制容量單位	
1 millilitre (ml) 毫升	
1 centilitre (ml) 厘升	=10 ml
1 decilitre (dl) 分升；公合	=10 cl
1 litre (l) 公升	=10 dl
1 decalitre (dal) 十升；公斗	=10 l
1 hectolitre (hl) 百升；公石	=10 dal
1 kilolitre (kl) 千升	=10 hl

- Normal Human Glucose Blood Test results should be 70–130 (mg / dl) before meals, and less than 180 mg / dl after meals. 人體的正常血糖含量必須維持在飯前 70 至 130 毫克每分升，飯後少於 180 毫克每分升。
- There are 400 calories in 1 litre Coke. 一公升的可樂含 400 卡路里。

2) 在英制中，最常用的容量單位是 pint（品脫）和 gallon（加侖）。

英制容量單位	
1 teaspoon 茶匙	
1 tablespoon 湯匙	= 3 teaspoons
1 cup 杯	= 16 tablespoons
1 pint 品脫	= 2 cups
1 quart 夸脫	= 2 pints
1 gallon 加侖	= 4 quarts

- A teaspoon of sugar weighs about four grams. 一茶匙的糖大概等於四克重量。
- a pint of milk 一品脫牛奶
- The average swimming pool takes 18,000–20,000 gallons of water to fill. 標準游泳池需要 18,000 至 20,000 加侖的水注滿。

⊕ **中英文比較**

中國傳統的容量單位為升、斗，多用來量米。成語「升斗市民」比喻那些為米飯奔波的小市民。

速度 (Speed)

1) 速度是描述物體運動快慢的物理量，在公制中常見的速度單位元是 metre per second（m / s；米每秒）和 kilometre per hour（km / hr；公里每小時）。

- The race car travels at 240 km per hour.
  那輛跑車的時速是每小時 240 公里。
- The speed of light is 199,792,458 m / s.
  光速是每秒 199,792,458 米。

2) 英式的速度計量單位元以 foot（英尺）和 mile（英里）來表示。

- foot per second 英尺每秒
- foot per minute 英尺每分鐘
- mile per hour (mph) 英里每小時
- 500 miles per day 每天 500 英里

3) 海里（sea mile; nautical mile）是航海上的長度單位，每小時航行 1 海里的速度叫做 1 節（knot）。

- The ship is moving at 10 nautical miles per hour. 船以每小時十海里的速度前進。
- The wind speed can be displayed in km / h, mph, m / s or knots. 風速可以公里 / 每小時、英里 / 每小時、英里 / 每秒或節來顯示。

溫度 (Temperature)

1) 氣溫即空氣的冷熱程度，以溫度計 (thermometer) 來量度，通常以攝氏度數 (degrees Celsius) 為單位，符號為 ℃。

- Water freezes at 0 degree Celsius / 0℃. 水在攝氏零度結冰。
- The normal temperature of the human body is 37℃. 人體的正常體溫是攝氏 37 度。

2) 零下的溫度 (sub-zero temperatures) 用 degrees below zero 或 degrees below freezing 來表示。

- It was six degrees below zero this morning. 今早的氣溫是零下六度。
- It's amazingly cold. It's like some 10 degrees below freezing. 冷得要命啊，有零下十度吧。

3) 現時全球大部份國家都使用攝氏溫標，只有少數國家 (如美國) 仍保留華氏溫標為法定計量單位。

- In New York, the warmest month of the year is July with an average maximum temperature of 82.50 degrees Fahrenheit. 在紐約，全年氣溫最高的月份為七月，平均最高溫度為華氏 82.5 度。

H **經緯度 (Latitude and longitude)**

經緯度是由經度與緯度的合稱而組成的一個坐標系統，能夠標示地球上任何一個位置。

緯度指某點與地球球心的連線和地球赤道面所成的線面角，其數值在 0 至 90 度之間。赤道的緯度是 0°，位於赤道以北的點的緯度叫北緯，記為 N，位於赤道以南的點的緯度稱南緯，記為 S。

不像緯度有赤道作為自然的起點，經度的起點定於英國格林維治（Greenwich）的本初子午線（prime meridian），其數值在 0 至 180 度之間。本初子午線的經度是 0°，位於本初子午線以東的點的經度叫東經，記為 E，位於本初子午線以東的點的經度叫西經，記為 W。

經緯度以度數（degree）表示，符號為 °，例如北京市的地理座標是：

- The latitude and longitude of Beijing is: 39° 54′ 20″ N, 116° 25′ 29″ E
  （讀：39 degrees 54 minutes 20 second NORTH and 116 degrees 25 minutes 29 seconds EAST）
  北京市位於北緯 39 度 54 分 20 秒，東經 116 度 25 分 29 秒之間。

注意，° 指 degree，′ 指 minute，″ 指 second。又如：

- Hong Kong Special Administrative Region lies between Latitude 22°08′ North and 22°35′ North, Longitude 113°49′ East and 114°31′ East.
  香港特別行政區位於北緯 22°08′ 至 22°35′ 及東經 113°49′ 至 114°31′ 之間。

12.2 速查表
Speed check

主要計算量度單位

Length 長度
公制
1 cm (centimetre) 厘米 = 10 mm (millimetres) 毫米
1 m (metre) 米 = 100 cm (centimetres) 厘米
1 km (kilometre) 公里；千米 = 1,000 m (metres) 米
英制
1 foot 英尺；呎 = 12 inches 英寸；吋
1 yard 碼 = 3 feet 英尺；呎
1 mile 英里；哩 = 1,760 yards 碼

Weight 重量
公制
1 kg (kilogram) 公斤；千克 = 1,000 g (grams) 克
英制
1 lb 磅 = 16 oz (ounces) 安士；盎司

Capacity 容量
1 l (litre) 升 = 1,000 ml (millilitres) 毫升

Temperature 重量
℉ (Fahrenheit) 華氏
冰點是 0℃ 或 32 ℉。水的沸點是
100℃ 或 212 ℉。

Section 2: Exercises

 數字練習

I. 寫出以下基數詞（cardinal numbers）的讀法：

1. 67

   _____

2. 243

   _____

3. 828

   _____

4. 1,705

   _____

5. 7,006

   _____

6. 49,220

   _____

   _____

7. 153,610

   _____

   _____

8. 2,225,525

   _____

   _____

   _____

9. 64,800,930

_____

_____

_____

10. 3,570,984,261

_____

_____

_____

II. 寫出以下讀法的基數詞：

1. Fifty-six

_____

2. Three hundred and twenty-two

_____

3. Nine hundred and sixty-nine

_____

4. One thousand one hundred and eleven

_____

5. Eight thousand and eighty-eight

_____

6. Seventy-two thousand five hundred and forty-one

   _____

7. One hundred and twenty-one thousand, three hundred and two

   _____

8. Three million, six hundred and twenty thousand, three hundred and seven

   _____

9. Eleven million, one hundred thousand, one hundred and one

   _____

10. Five billion, six hundred and eight million, two hundred and forty-two thousand, six hundred and twelve

   _____

III. 寫出以下序數詞（ordinal numbers）的讀法：

1. 3rd

   _____

2. 22nd

   _____

3. 40th

   _____

4. 83th

_____

5. 90th

_____

6. 100th

_____

7. 361st

_____

8. 20,000th

_____

9. 44,333,222nd

_____

10. 700,000,000th

_____

IV. 用羅馬數字（Roman Numerals）寫出以下數字：

1. 3

   _____

2. 22

   _____

3. 40

   _____

4. 83

   _____

5. 90

   _____

6. 100

   _____

7. 361

   _____

8. 1997

   _____

9. 2014

   _____

10. 3535

   _____

V. 用數字（Roman Numerals）寫出以下羅馬數字：

1. VII

   _____

2. XXXVII

   _____

3. LV

   _____

4. LXIX

   _____

5. XCII

   _____

6. CXXX

   _____

7. CD

   _____

8. DXXIII

   _____

9. MM

   _____

10. MMMCMXCIX

   _____

VI. 寫出以下份數（fractions）的讀法：

1. ½

_____

2. ⅓

_____

3. 16 ¼

_____

4. 33 ⅜

_____

5. 75 ⅑

_____

VII. 寫出以下讀法的份數：

1. One fifth

_____

2. Six and one tenth

_____

3. Nine and three quarters

_____

4. Fifteen and one ninth

_____

5. Thirty-six and two thirds

_____

VIII. 寫出以下小數（decimals）和百份數（percentages）的讀法：

1. 0.5

_____

2. 0.025

_____

3. 4.628

_____

4. 99.9

_____

5. 137.02

_____

6. 0.63%

_____

7. 9%

_____

8. 19.34%

_____

9. 100%

_____

10. 150%

_____

IX. 寫出以下運算 (calculations) 的讀法:

加數

1. 9 + 9 = 18

_____

2. 125 + 343 = 468

_____

_____

減數

3. 13 − 6 = 7

_____

4. 696 - 232 = 464

_____

乘數

5. 7 x 3 = 21

_____

6. 24 x 220 = 5,280

_____

_____

除數

7. 24 ÷ 6 = 4

_____

8. 1,664 ÷ 13 = 128

_____

_____

X. 寫出以下號碼的常用讀法：

電話號碼

1. 3779 9332

2. 6999 8801

信用卡號碼

3. 3087 7065 5200 8000

Section 3: Integrated Sentence Exercises

 綜合句子練習

I. 選擇題。

1. Virginia is (A. seventeen B. of seventeen C. at seventeen).

2. This old tree is (A. three hundreds B. three hundred C. three hundred years old).

3. My grand-grandfather is (A. 101 years B. one hundred and one year C. one hundred one years) old.

4. That woman must be in (A. the late sixties B. her late sixties C. late sixties).

5. These stories are written for children (A. age B. ageing C. aged) 10 or above.

6. Harry is a young British man (A. at B. of C. in) twenty-nine.

7. She is an old woman (A. about B. of about C. in about) seventy.

8. A (A. ten-weeks-old B. ten weeks old C. ten-week-old) dolphin was washed up dead on Lantau shores.

9. HK$100 stands for (A. Hong Kong one hundred dollars B. one hundred Hong Kong dollars C. Hong Kong one-hundred-dollar).

10. 'How was your recent trip to South Korea?'

    'It was great. We visited (A. five-friend B. 5 friends C. five friends) in Seoul, and spent the (A. two last days B. last two days C. last two-day) at Busan.'

II. 改正以下句子。（提示：每句中有一個錯處。）

1. Is it good to give solid food to babies under six months in age?
2. A woman ageing 60 has given birth to twins.
3. Girl ages between 13 to 18 are most at risk from sexual harassment.
4. He died at the age ninety.
5. This temple is more than one hundred and fifty years ago.
6. She became a professor at age of twenty-seven.
7. There are thirty-three ten-years-old in this class.
8. She came the third in Maths.
9. He has spent several million of dollars on this sports car.
10. She was born on the 8th July, 1992.

III. 翻譯以下句子。

1. 我早上通常八點起來。

   _____

2. 她身高 5 英尺 2 英寸。

   _____

3. 她的體重是 48 公斤。

   _____

4. 太平山的高度為 552 米。

   _____

5. 他的科學得了 83 分。

   _____

6. 她以 11 比 7 贏了第一盤（局）。

   _____

7. 她代表學校參加女子 200 米自由泳。

   _____

8. 我會參加男子 200 米跨欄。

   _____

9. 你最好在一小時十五分鐘內完成你的家課。

   _____

10. 香港有 720 萬人口。

    _____

11. 他們一見鍾情。

    _____

12. 劉邦成為了漢朝（公元前 206 年—公元 220 年）的首位皇帝。

    _____

13. 水在攝氏零度結冰。

14. 這睡房的面積是 120 平方英尺。

15. 香港的位置介乎北緯 22 度 15 分，東經 114 度 10 分之間。

Section 4: Integrated Contextual Exercises

 綜合篇章練習

I. 填充題：根據上下文填入適當字眼。注意：每個詞語只能用一次。

One-litre   25   250   2013   XXXIV   Room 1603   16/F

1.( ) November, 2014
Marketing and Sales Department
ABC Corporation
2.( ), **3.**( ), Sing Kung Commercial Bldg,
188 Queen's Road East,
Central,
Hong Kong

Dear Sir or Madam,

You have previously supplied us with crockery and we should be glad if you would now quote for the items named below, manufactured by the Wei Wei Pottery
Company of Fujian. The pattern we require is listed in your **4.**( ) catalogue as **5.**( ) Conway Spot (Green)'

6.( ) Teacups and Saucers
250 Tea Plates
7. 30 ( ) Teapots

Prices quoted should include packing and delivery to the above address.

When replying please also state discounts allowable, terms of payment and earliest possible date of delivery.

Yours faithfully,
Jennifer Kong

II. 選擇題：

1.(A. 28 November, B. 28 November C. 28th November) 2014

Dear Ms Kong,

CONWAY SPOT (GREEN) GILT RIMS

Thank you for your enquiry of **2.**(A. 25 November B. Nov 25 C. 25th Nov,) for a further supply of our crockery. We are pleased to quote as follows:

Teacups	$535 per **3.**(A. a hundred B. hundred C. hundreds)
Tea Saucers	**4.**(A. $400 B. $4 hundred C. 400 dollars) per hundred
Tea Plates	$420 per hundred
Teapots	$23 **5.**(A. one B. per C. each)

These prices include packing and delivery, but crates are charged for, with an allowance for their return in good condition.

We can deliver from stock and will allow you a discount of **6.**(A. 5% B. five percentage C. five%), but only on items ordered in quantities of **7.**(A. two hundreds B. 200 C. two-hundred) or more. In addition, there would be a cash discount of 1.5% on total cost of payment within **8.**(A. 1st B. first C. one) month from date of invoice.

We hope you will find these terms satisfactory and look forward to the pleasure of your order.

Yours sincerely,

Joseph W. K. Wang
Marketing Director

III. 選擇題：

Thanksgiving Day

In the **1.**(A. mid-19th B. middle-19th C. middle nineteenth) century some American people began to promote the idea of a national Thanksgiving Day. In **2.**(A. eighteen sixty-three B. one thousand eight hundred and sixty-three C. 1863), during the American Civil War, President Abraham Lincoln proclaimed the last Thursday in November as 'a day of thanksgiving and praise to our beneficent Father'. Each year afterwards, for **3.**(A. seventy five B. 75 C. three-quarter) years, the President formally proclaimed that Thanksgiving Day should be celebrated on the last Thursday of November.

In 1939 U.S. President Franklin Roosevelt shifted the day of Thanksgiving from the last Thursday in November to **4.**(A. one B. first C. an) week earlier. He wanted to help business by allowing for an extra week of shopping between Thanksgiving and Christmas. Many Americans objected to the change in their holiday customs and continued to celebrate Thanksgiving on the last Thursday of the month. In May 1941 Roosevelt admitted that he had made a mistake and signed a bill that established the **5.**(A. fourth B. 4th C. four) Thursday of November as the national Thanksgiving holiday, which it has been ever since.

During the **6.**(A. twenty B. twentieth C. 20th) century, the day after Thanksgiving gradually became known as the **7.**(A. 1st B. first C. one) day of Christmas shopping season. To attract customers, large retailers began to sponsor lavish parades with richly decorated floats and gigantic balloons on Thanksgiving Day, and the parades attract **8.**(A. million B. millions C. 1,000,000) of spectators each year.

IV. 改正錯處：找出 10 個錯處，然後作出改正。

Witnesses of a UFO crash

It was late in the day, just before 5 o'clock in the afternoon, on five December 1965, when a fireball flashed through the evening sky. It was seen 1st over Canada, then by thousand in Michigan and Ohio. Over the northern edge of Ohio, near Cleveland, it might have made a slight turn, and then it headed southeast, towards Pennsylvania.

At 4.47 P.M., the object struck the ground southeast of Pittsburg, near the small town of Kecksburg. In its wake it had left thousands of stunned witnesses, and debris reported to have fallen from it started fires near Elyria, Ohio.

Frances Kalp was interviewed for the breaking story of the object. She told the news director that the object had crashed into the woods near her home. Her children wanted to walk down to where her son said he'd seen 'a star on fire.' Kalp caught the children about one and a ½ mile from the crash site. There was smoke climbing out of the trees, and there was a bright object off to 1 side. Kalp said that it was like 'a 4 pointed star.'

But Kalp was not the only person to see the object in the air. Bob Blystone, who was fifteenth in 1965, saw what he described as an orange jet trail at low altitude. He drove down to the Kecksburg area. He was there when 2 state police cars arrived.

V. 改正錯處：找出 10 個錯處，然後作出改正。

The Titanic

It's been over one-hundred-years since the Titanic sank on its maiden voyage.

After the sinking of the *Titanic* on 1912, April 15, the great ship slumbered on the floor of the Atlantic Ocean for over 70 years before its wreckage was discovered. On September 1,1985, a joint American-French expedition, headed by famous American oceanographer Dr. Robert Ballard, found the *Titanic* over two miles below the ocean's surface by using an unmanned submersible called *Argo*. This discovery gave new meaning to the *Titanic's* sinking and gave birth to new dreams in ocean exploration.

Built in Ireland from 1,909 to 1,912 on behalf of the British-owned White Star Line, the *Titanic* officially left its final European port of Queenstown, Ireland on April 11, 1912. Carrying over 2200 passengers and crew, the *Titanic* began its maiden voyage across the Atlantic, headed for New York.

The *Titanic* carried passengers from all walks of life. Tickets were sold to first, 2nd, and third class passengers; the latter group largely consisting of immigrants seeking a better life.

Only 3 days after setting sail, the *Titanic* struck the iceberg at 1140 p.m. on April 14 1912, somewhere in the North Atlantic. Although it took the ship over two and ½ hours to sink, the vast majority of the crew and passengers perished due to a significant lack of lifeboats and improper use of those that did exist. The lifeboats could have held over 1,100 people, but only seven hundred and five people were saved; nearly 1,500 perished the night the *Titanic* sank.

(Extract from: *Jennifer L. Goss: Discovery of the Titanic Shipwreck*)

Section 5: Creative Writing Exercises

 創意寫作：看漫畫，寫故事，想數詞

Exercise 01

The Jupiter

請按每格的提示文字,以 60 字為限,運用正確數詞寫出故事。

Jupiter, planet from the Sun, solar system

diameter, at its equator

atmosphere, hydrogen, helium, by mass

moons, be discovered, Galileo Galilei, 1610

Exercise 02

My great-grandmother

請按每格的提示文字，以 50 字為限，運用正確數詞寫出故事。

Great-grandma, teens,
move, Hong Kong, China

marry, only 16

husband, die, war, break out, '40s

birthday, today, eighties, still,
active, strong

_____

_____

_____

_____

_____

_____

Exercise 03

My classmate

請按每格的提示文字，以 50 字為限，運用正確數詞寫出故事。

¹⁄₁₀, classmate, new immigrant, Xiaoming

like, sit, first row

come first, Putonghua, 99%, last test

like, sports, school record, men's 200 m hurdles

_____

_____

_____

_____

_____

_____

_____

Exercise 04

King Cobra snake

請按每格的提示文字，以 50 字為限，運用正確數詞寫出故事。

king cobra, largest, venomous, world
Xiaoming

grow, as long as

shed, 4–6 times, live up to, 20 years

single bite, kill, 20 grown men

Section 6: Advanced Level

 進階：數詞的語法功能、相關成語

6.1 Numerals and grammar 數詞的語法功能

一）數詞的語序（position）

1) 數字與限定詞（determiner）

數字與限定詞 * 連用來修飾名詞時，數字必須置於限定詞之後。

⊕ **定冠詞（the）**

例
- the three children 三個孩子

⊕ **指示代詞（these, those）**

例
- these three children 這三個孩子

⊕ **名詞所有格（Bob's, Christine's, his friend's, etc.）**

例
- Liz's three children 麗絲的三個孩子

⊕ **所有格形容詞（my, your, his, her, their）**

例
- her three children 她的三個孩子

⊕ **前限定詞（all, both, half）**

例
- all three children 全部三個孩子

---

* 限定詞（determiner）用來限定名詞所指的範圍，如使名詞變成泛指、特指或說明數量。數詞（number）本身就是限定詞的一種，除了數詞以外，英語中的限定詞還包括冠詞（article）、指示代詞（demonstrative）、名詞所有格（possessive noun）、所有格形容詞（possessive adjective）、數量詞（quantifier）與某些形容詞性的物主代詞。

⊕ **序數和基數共同修飾一名詞時，序數要放在基數之前。**

- the first five newcomers 首五個新加入的人
- the last two weeks 最後兩個星期
- The first two lessons on Monday are Maths and Chinese.
  星期一的頭兩課是數學和中文。
- They spent the last five days of the summer holidays in
  Maldives. 他們在馬爾代夫度過了暑假的最後五天。

2) 數字與形容詞

數字與形容詞連用來修飾名詞時，數字必須置於形容詞之前。

- Three Little Pigs 三隻小豬
- her two small children 她的兩個孩子
- five beautiful fairies 五個漂亮的仙女

二) 主謂一致（agreement）

主謂一致指 "人稱" 和 "數" 方面的一致關係。

⊕ 複數主詞需要複數動詞

• At least three people were killed in the bomb blasts. 爆炸中至少有三人死亡。

當 there be 句型的主語是一系列事物時，謂語應與最鄰近的主語保持一致。

• There is a pen and three books on the desk. 書桌上有一支筆和三本書。
• There are three books and a pen on the desk. 書桌上有三本書和一支筆。

• There are thirty-nine boys and only one girl in this class. 這個班裏有三十九名男生，只有一名女生。
• There is one girl and thirty-nine boys in this class. 這班有一名女生和三十九名男生。

除此之外，在由 not only...but also... 、 not just...but... 、 or 、 either...or... 、 neither...nor... 連接主語的句型中，謂語動詞的單複數也是按「就近原則」處理，即按與謂語動詞最靠近的那個主語，來確定謂語動詞的單複數形式。

• Either you or she is to go. 你或者她去。
• Not only John but also I am going to Beijing next week. 除了約翰，我也會在下星期去北京。
• Neither Aunt Jenny nor her three children are at home. 珍妮姨姨和她的三個孩子都不在家。

⊕ **謂語動詞與前面的主語一致**

當主語後面跟有 with、together with、like、except、but、no less than、as well as 等詞引起的短語時,謂語動詞與前面的主語一致。

- The teacher together with ten students is visiting the museum. 老師連同十個學生一起參觀博物館。
- He as well as his three children wants to go boating. 他和他三個孩子都想去划船。

⊕ **謂語需用單數**

當主語是一本書或一條格言時,謂語動詞常用單數。

- *Snow White and the Seven Dwarfs is* a book known to lovers of fairy tales.《白雪公主與七個小矮人》是童話愛好者熟悉的一本好書。

表示金錢、時間、距離、價格或度量衡的複合名詞作主語時,通常把這些名詞看作一個整體,謂語一般用單數(用複數也可,意思不變)。

- Ten yuan is enough. 十元夠了。
- Three weeks was allowed for making the necessary preparations. 有三個星期來做準備工夫。

三）數字作複合形容詞（numbers in compound adjectives）

由 "數字 + 名詞" 結合而成複合形容詞，可分為以下幾類：

✚ 數字 + 單數名詞

- one-horse race 看來某人可以輕易獲勝的比賽
- one-man business 一人經營的公司
- one-man band 單人樂隊；一人組織 / 活動
- one-night stand 一夜情
- one-parent family (= single-parent family) 單親家庭
- one-way ticket 單程車票
- two-month maternity leave 兩個月的產假
- three-day event 馬術三日賽
- three-piece suit 三件套的衣服（包括上衣、馬甲和褲子）
- four-leaf clover 四葉草
- four-letter word 粗話；髒詞
- four-poster bed 四柱大牀
- four-star general（美國陸軍）四星上將
- five-star hotel 五星級酒店
- seventy-storey building 七十層高的大廈
- Marriage has to be a two-way street. 婚姻中夫妻雙方應互諒互讓。
- It's a five-minute walk from here to my office. 從這兒到我的辦公室要走五分鐘的路。
- Her two-year certificate of deposit carries an interest rate of 3.9 percent. 她的兩年期定期存款有 3.9% 的利息回報。
- I stayed up late last night in order to turn in a fifty-page report. 我昨天很晚才睡，為了趕完一份五十頁的報告。

⊕ 數字 + 單數名詞 + ed

- one-eyed dragon 獨眼龍 (i.e. a dragon with one eye)
- one-legged girl 單腳少女
- one-armed bandit 吃角子老虎機 (= slot machine)
- one-armed swordsman 獨臂劍客
- three-cornered fight 三方角逐
- three-legged race 二人三足賽跑
- two-handed catch 雙手接球
- two-sided problem 雙重問題
- four-pointed star 四角星
- The newspapers give a very one-sided account of the war.
  報紙對這場戰爭作了非常片面的報導。

※ 注意，在這一類的用法中，數字 one 可以用形容詞代替，例如 a round-faced woman、a long-armed ape, a green-eyed monster。

⊕ 數字 + 單數名詞 + 形容詞

- a two-month-old baby 兩個月大的嬰兒
- a twelve-year-old boy 十二歲的男孩
- a 50-metre-wide river 河寬 50 米的河流

應當注意的是，有連字號時前置，不管數字是多少，名詞要用單數，後置定語時去掉連字號，名詞用複數。比較以下兩組句子：

- Colin has a five-year-old sister. 科倫有一個五歲大的姐妹。
  （用作前置定語，名詞 year 要用單數）
- Colin has a sister of five years old. 科倫有一個五歲大的姐妹。
  （用作後置定語，名詞 year 要用複數）

- They built a three-hundred-metre-long bridge across the river.
  他們在河上築起了一條三百米長的橋。
  （用作前置定語，名詞 metre 要用單數）
- They built a bridge of three hundred metres across the river.
  他們在河上築起了一條三百米長的橋。
  （用作後置定語，名詞 metre 要用複數）

6.2 Rules for writing numbers 數詞的寫作規則

在圖書、報紙、期刊等出版物中，數字使用的頻率很高，如果對數字的用法沒有統一標準，這不僅使編輯、排版、校對工作增加了麻煩，同時也會造成閱讀與理解上之困難。以下為書寫數字時的一般寫作規則，可作參考。

➕ **1 至 10 用單詞表示，10 以上的數目用阿拉伯數字。**

- She has two brothers and three sisters. 她有兩個兄弟三個姐妹。
- The group of eight boarded the ship in Nanjing and stayed in first class. 一行八人於南京登船並入住頭等艙。
- The death toll in the ship capsize in Yangtze river, China's worst shipping disaster in 70 years, rose to 434 after two more bodies were found this morning. 這次中國長江船難是 70 年來最嚴重的一次，繼今早再發現兩具屍體後，死亡人數上升至 434 人。

※ 注意，如數字以清單或列表形式出現，必須統一寫法。

- ✗ They have four children aged six, eight, 12, and 14.
- ✓ They have four children aged 6, 8, 12, and 14.
  他們有四個孩子，分別是 6 歲、8 歲、12 歲和 14 歲。

- ✗ We will stay here for 2 or three weeks.
- ✓ We will stay here for two or three weeks.
  我們會在這裏逗留兩至三星期。

如句子短小，有些作者喜歡用單詞來表示數目。

➕ **比較**

- ✗ She is 11.
- ✓ She is eleven.

- ✗ Can you lend me 100 dollars?
- ✓ Can you lend me a hundred dollars?

※ 注意，也有些人 1 至 100 用單詞表示，100 以上才用阿拉伯數字；使用者須靈活處理並自行決定，只求全篇體例統一便可。

⊕ 句首不用阿拉伯數字。

例
× 434 people died in the shipwreck.
✓ Four hundred and thirty-four people died in the shipwreck.
沉船意外中 434 人喪生。

例
× 1st July is an important date in Hong Kong history.
✓ The first of July is an important date in Hong Kong history.
七月一日是香港歷史上重要的一天。

例
× 27 students took part in the singing contest.
✓ Twenty-seven students took part in the singing contest.
二十七名學生參加了歌唱比賽。

例
× 52% of Hong Kong people live in the New Territories.
✓ Fifty-two percent of Hong Kong people live in the New Territories. 在香港，百分之五十二的人口居於新界。

※ 注意，句首數目用單詞，句中數目則可用數字表示。

例
• Sixty-eight students participated last year, but there were 96 this year. 去年有 68 個學生參加，今年卻有 96 個。
• Sixty-five-year-old passenger Zhu Dawen and 21-year-old sailor Chen Xiaoming are the only two survivors who were saved from the sunken ship. 沉船意外中被救獲的兩名生還者是 65 歲的乘客朱大文和 21 歲的船員陳小明。

※ 注意，年份與標題則屬除外。

例
× Nineteen ninety-seven was a memorable year in Hong Kong history.
✓ 1997 was a memorable year in Hong Kong history.
1997 是香港歷史上富有紀念價值的一年。

例
× Four Hundred and Thirty-four Died in Shipwreck
✓ 434 Died in Shipwreck
沉船意外 434 人死

⊕ **具體數目用阿拉伯數字表示顯得更簡潔明瞭。**

- A Chinese billionaire took 6,400 employees on a trip to France. He booked up 140 hotels in Paris and 4,760 rooms in 79 four- and five-star hotels in Cannes and Monaco. 一位中國億萬富翁帶領 6,400 名員工遊覽法國，一口氣訂下巴黎 140 家酒店，並在康城和摩納哥訂下了 79 家四至五星級酒店的 4,760 間套房。
- 8,943 people were killed in the tsunami, and 467,856 people were displaced.
  8,943 人在海嘯中喪生，467,858 人則無家可歸。

但不定數量、近似值用單詞表示較恰當。

- a few hundred miles 幾百公里
- Many thousands were killed in the tsunami, and about half a million were displaced. 數以千計人在海嘯中喪生，約五十萬人則無家可歸。

⊕ **遇上百萬以上的大數目時，如是具體數目用阿拉伯數字表示。**

- The sales turnover last month was $3,520,650. 上月的銷售額為 $3,520,650。
- In 2011, the population in Hong Kong was 7,071,576.
  2011 年，香港的人口為 7,071,576。

大整數用單詞（或數字加單詞）來表示較恰當。

- There were six million visitors last year. 去年有六百萬名遊客。
- The population in China is just over 1.4 billion. 中國人口剛剛超過 14 億。
- The profit rose to $6 million in the first quarter of the year.
  今年第一季度之利潤上升至 600 萬元。

※ 注意用法必須統一。

- ✗ You can earn from one million dollars to 3 million dollars.
- ✗ You can earn from $1 million to three million dollars.
- ✓ You can earn from one million to three million dollars.

⊕ **遇到份數，可用帶連字號的單詞表示。**

- About one-eight of the class comes from China. 班上大約八份之一的學生來自中國。
- One-half is slightly less than two-thirds. 二份之一略少於三份之二。

帶份數則例外，必須以數字寫出。

- The recipe calls for 1½ cups whole milk and ½ cup honey. 食譜要求 1.5 杯全脂牛奶和 1/2 杯蜂蜜。
- They expect a 4½ percent wage increase. 他們希望加薪 4.5%。

帶份數出現在句首時則作別論。

× 4½ percent was the expected wage increase.
✓ Four and one half percent was the expected wage increase. 加薪幅度要求是 4.5%。

⊕ **百份數用阿拉伯數字表示。**

- In 2013, 14% of the population in Hong Kong were 65 and above.
2013 年，香港人口中有 14% 為 65 歲或以上的長者。

百份數出現在句首時則作別論。

- Fourteen percent of the population in Hong Kong were 65 and above.
香港人口中有 14% 為 65 歲或以上的長者。

⊕ **小數用阿拉伯數字表示，除非用於句首（這情況並不常見）。**

- The normal body temperature is 98.6°F (37℃). 正常體溫是 98.6°F（37℃）。
- Pi (π) has a value of 3.141, to three decimals. 圓周率 π 的三位小數近似值為 3.141。

小數出現在直接引語（direct speech）時則屬例外。

- He held the thermometer up and said, 'Thirty-seven degree Celsius. Normal.' 他拿起溫度計看，然後說：「攝氏 37 度。正常。」

純小數必須寫出小數點前用以定位的 0。

- ✗ How long does it take to drive .6 miles at 60 mph.
- ✓ How long does it take to drive 0.6 miles at 60 mph. 以時速 60 英里來算，走 0.6 英里路的話要多長時間？

少於一元的幣值不宜用小數標示。

- ✗ It costs only $0.80.
- ✓ It costs only eighty cents / 80 cents. 成本只需八毛錢。

⊕ **具統計意義（如計量單位、統計數據等）者，使用阿拉伯數字。**

- 70 km per hour 每小時 70 公里
- a discount of 10 percent 九折
- Add 2 cups of brown rice. 加入兩杯糙米。
- The screen is 48 inches wide and 36 inches tall. 螢幕為 48 英寸寬、36 英寸高。
- She bought 7 yards of silk. 她買了七碼絲綢。
- He ordered 3 pounds of smoked salmon. 他訂購了三磅醃三文魚。
- a capacity of 3.8 litres and a power output of 136 kilowatts at 3,900 revolutions per minute 容積為 3.8 升，轉速為每分鐘 3,900 轉，時輸出功率是 136 千瓦

如果涉及的數目和單位是不定數，可用單詞表示。

- about five miles per hour 每小時大約 5 英里
- at least ten metres away 至少有 10 米遠
- hesitated for a moment or two 猶豫了片刻
- I have warned you a hundred times. 我已經警告你不知多少

遍了。

⊕ **兩個數字同時出現時，可分別以數字或詞語表示，以免混淆。**

例 | × There are 10 13-year-olds in this class.
✓ There are ten 13-year-olds in this class.
這班有十個 13 歲學生。

例 | × These are the top 10 5-star hotels in the city.
✓ These are the top 10 five-star hotels in the city.
這是市內最好的十家五星級酒店。

⊕ **時間、日期用阿拉伯數字表示。**

例 | • The flight leaves at 9:45 p.m. 航班於晚上 9 時 45 分出發。
• Please arrive by 2:30 sharp. 請務必在兩點半到達。

如果用 o'clock 來表示時間，一般用單詞。

例 | • It's ten o'clock. 十點。
• It's a quarter to eight. 七點四十五分。

⊕ **日期‧年代等用阿拉伯數字表示。**

例 | × The Rosewell Incident took place on the eighth of July, 1947.
✓ The Rosewell Incident took place on 8 July, 1947.
羅茲威爾事件發生在 1947 年 7 月 8 日。

十年期（decade）可用單詞表示，但不用大寫。

例 | × The electronics industry started to blossom in the Sixties.
✓ The electronics industry started to blossom in the sixties.
電子業在六十年代興起。

也可用數字表示。

例 | ✓ The electronics industry started to blossom in the '60s.

✓ The electronics industry started to blossom in the 1960s.

⊕ **具一般數字意義（如身份證號碼、編號、序數、電話、郵遞區號、街道號、門牌號碼等）者，使用阿拉伯數字。**

例
- His ID number is G563 095(4). 他的身份證號碼是 G563 095(4)。
- Chapter 3 of this book begins on page 48. 本書第三章從 48 頁開始。
- The Wangs live on the 30th floor at 88 Nathan Road in Tsimshatsui. 王先生一家住在尖沙咀彌敦道 88 號 30 樓。

例
- ✗ Please wait outside Room Fourteen.
- ✓ Please wait outside Room 14.
  請在 14 房間門口等候。

⊕ **數字用語屬描述性用語、專有名詞（如地名、書名、店名等）或慣用語者，一律使用單詞。**

例
- ✗ A Tale of 2 Cities
- ✓ A Tale of Two Cities
  《雙城記》

例
- ✗ Michelle Obama is the 44th 1st lady of the United States.
- ✓ Michelle Obama is the 44th first lady of the United States.
  米歇爾・奧巴馬是美國第四十四個第一夫人。

例
- ✗ Our team won after we scored a goal at the 11th hour.
- ✓ Our team won after we scored a goal at the eleventh hour.
  我隊在最後一刻入球勝出。

6.3 Number idioms 英語中與數字有關的成語

一）one

1. **a quick one**【非正式】匆匆一口喝下的酒：How about **a quick one** at the pub? 去酒吧喝一杯怎麼樣？

2. **all in one** 兼具數種用途或功能：It's a printer, scanner, copier and fax **all in one.** 它集列印機、掃描機、影印機、傳真機多種功能於一身。

3. **all rolled into one** 身兼兩職或數職：She is a mother, actress and Legco councillor **all rolled into one.** 她身兼母親演員與立法會議員三職。

4. **at one time** 曾經；過去某個時期：**At one time** he was a drug addict but now he has become an anti-drug activist. 他曾經是個癮君子，現在卻致力打擊毒害。

5. **back to square one** 退回起點；重頭再來：Negotiations collapsed, so **back to square one.** 談判失敗，所以要重頭再來。

6. **be at one with** ①【稍微正式】與某人看法或意見一致：I'm completely **at one with** you on this decision. 就在這個決定上，我跟你的看法完全一致。② 與環境成為一體：I feel peaceful and **at one with** nature. 我感到平和，和大自然融為一體。

7. **for one thing** 首先；其一（用來列舉理由）：I don't think I can help you. **For one thing,** the pay is low. For another, I'm simply not interested. 我該幫不上忙了，首先，費用太低了，其次，我根本沒興趣。

8. **I, for one, ...** 就拿我自己來說吧（強調自己相信或會做某事，並希望其他人也一樣）：**I, for one,** believe in extraterrestrial life. 我自己就很相信有外星生物。

9. **look after / take care of number one**【口】只顧自己（多用來指人自私）：You gotta **look after** number one, right? 你只顧自己，是吧？/ She **takes care of number one** and never thinks about anyone else.

10. one and only 聞名的；知名的：He's the one and only Kim Soohyun! 他就是無人不知的金秀賢！

11. **number one** ① 頭號；最成功的；第一：She used to be the **number one** model in Hong Kong. 她曾經是香港首席名模。②【口】小便；尿尿（尤對兒童所說的委婉語）：I drank way too much soda, I need to go **number**

one. 我喝了太多汽水，要去上小號。〈另見〉31 number two

12. **one and the same** 同一個；完全一樣：To my surprise, David's girlfriend and Bill's sister are **one and the same**. 讓我頗感意外的是，大衛的女友和比爾的姐姐原來是同一個人。

13. **one for the road**【非正式】臨別前的最後一杯酒：Before I left, he persuaded me to have **one for the road**. 我打算離開了，他還是要我多喝最後一杯才走。

14. **one good turn deserves another** 投桃報李；善有善報：He fixed my computer so I took him to a 3D movie. **One good turn deserves another**. 他幫我修理電腦，我帶他去看 3D 電影，禮尚往來嘛。

15. **one in a million** ①【非正式】了不起的人；獨一無二，無與倫比的人：She's fantastic. She's **one in a million** 她這個人真好，那是萬中無一。② 微乎其微（的機會）：Don't worry. The chances of anything going wrong are **one in a million**. 放心，出錯的機會微乎其微。

16. **one of the boys** 某一群體中與其他人打成一片的人：Our boss tries to be **one of the boys** but actually nobody likes him. 老闆想跟我們打成一片，可是我們沒有人喜歡他。

17. **one of these days** 不久：You're going to get into troubles **one of these days**. 你很快就會出事的。

18. **one of those days** 諸事不順，甚麼都不對勁的一天：It's just been **one of those days**. 多倒楣的一天。

19. **one of those things** 必須接受的事；不可避免的事：Her sudden illness is **one of those things** and there is nothing we can do about it. 她突然患病，這是命中註定的，我們做不了甚麼。

20. **one too many**【非正式】飲酒過量；足以使人喝醉的一杯：Don't drive if you've had **one too many**. 喝多了就別開車。

21. **one-to-one** 一對一：I need to discuss it with you **one-to-one**. 我需要和你單獨商量這事情。

22. **one or two** (= a few) 一兩個；幾個；少數：There are **one or two** things I want to tell you before I leave. 我走之前還有一兩件事要跟你講。

23. **pull a fast one** 欺騙；詐欺：He's **pulling a fast one** when he said he had a stomachache and went home. 他使詐，這邊喊肚子疼，那邊就溜回家去了。

24. **put one over on someone**【非正式】哄騙某人：Don't try to **put one over on me!** 別想騙我！

25. **That's a new one on me**【非正式】對我是新鮮事；對我是前所未見的東西：`Jennifer has come out to her parents.'`Really! **That's a new one on me.'**「珍妮花向她的父母出櫃了。」「真的！這件事我才第一次聽到。」

26. **the one that got away** 未能得到而難以忘懷的寶貴事物；未能把握的成功機會：I should've treated him better, he's definitely **the one that got away.** 我早就應該對他好一點，現在失之交臂，讓我念念不忘。

27. **There's one born every minute** 總會有人受騙上當的；笨蛋無處不在：She played all the time and then wondered why she'd failed the exams! **There's one born every minute,** isn't there? 她整天只顧玩樂，還在問為何自己會考試失敗，有沒有這麼一個蠢材？

二）two

28. **in two minds** 三心兩意；猶豫不決：I was **in two minds** whether or not to go to her wedding banquet. 要不要去她的婚宴，我真是拿不定主意。

29. **in two shakes** (of a lamb's tail)【舊；非正式】馬上；很快：I'll catch up with you guys **in two shakes.** 我馬上趕上來了。

30. **kill two birds with one stone** 一石二鳥；一箭雙雕；一舉兩得：I **killed two birds with one stone** and bought the tickets on the way to see grandma. 我去見外婆時順道買了門票，真是一舉兩得。

31. **number two**【口】大便；出恭（尤對兒童所說的委婉語）：Had so much to eat, gotta do a massive **number two.** 吃太多了，要去上大號了。〈另見〉11 number one

32. **put two and two together**【非正式】根據事實推斷或臆測：`How did you know he's the guy who'd stolen my phone?'``I'd seen him come close to you a couple of times so I just **put two and two together.'**「你怎麼知道他就是偷我電話的人？」「推斷吧，因為我見到他有好幾次走到妳身旁。」

33. **that makes two of us**【口】我們兩人的情況一樣：`But I don't know anything about cooking.'``Well, that makes two of us.'**「可是我對烹飪一竅不通。」「是呀，我跟你一樣。」

34. **there's no two ways about it**【口】別無選擇;毫無疑問:You have to go to see her whether you like it or not. **There's no two ways about it.** 你喜歡也好不喜歡也好,你得要去見她,別無選擇。

35. **two company, three's a crowd** 兩人成伴,三人不歡:'Can I go to lunch with you and Angela?' 'Well, **two's company, three's a crowd.**'「我可以跟你喝安琪兒一起吃午飯嗎?」「這樣嘛,兩個人剛好,三個人太擠了。」

36. **two heads are better than one** 人多智廣;三個臭皮匠勝過一個諸葛亮:Come over here and help me solve these maths questions. **Two heads are better than one.** 過來一下,幫我解答這些數學題。一人計短,二人計長。

37. **two wrongs don't make a right** 兩個錯誤並不等於一個正確;不能利用別人的錯誤來掩飾自己的錯誤:Don't fight back, Eric. **Two wrongs don't make a right.** 不要還擊了,埃里克冤冤相報何時了?

三) three to ten

38. **give three cheers** 讚許;表揚;歡呼,喝彩:The crowd **gave three cheers** for their team. 群眾向他們的球隊歡呼喝彩。

39. **the three R's**【非正式】初等教育的三要素:Reading(讀)、wRiting(寫)、aRithmetic(算):This study looks into how children learn about **the three R's.** 這項研究分析孩童如何掌握讀寫算三項技能。

40. **on all fours** 匍匐着;爬着:You'll have to get down **on all fours** to go into the hole. 你要俯身爬下來才能進入那洞口。

41. **five o'clock shadow**(早上刮過後當天又長出的)短鬍子茬兒:He looks like a mess, but it is mostly because of his **five o'clock shadow.** 他看上去很邋遢,那是因為他臉上長了鬍子茬兒。

42. **give someone five** 與某人擊掌(表示對某事很滿意):He **gave me five** when he passed in the corridor. 他在走廊經過時與我擊掌。

43. **at sixes and sevens** 亂七八糟:Kelly is always **at sixes and sevens** when she's home by herself. 凱莉獨自在家的時候總是亂七八糟。

44. **six feet under** 墓木已拱:The old man died last week and is **six feet under** now. 那老翁上星期過身,現在已入土為安。

45. **six of one, half a dozen the other**【喻】半斤八兩;不相上下:She's always accusing her boyfriend of picking a quarrel, but if you ask me, it's

six of one and half a dozen of the other. 她經常指責男友故意挑剔，如果你問我，我會說他們兩個只是半斤八兩。

46. **in seventh heaven**【幽默】處於無比的快樂中；快樂極了：Since they lived together they've been **in seventh heaven**. 他們同居以後就一直過得逍遙快活。

47. **have one over the eight**【英；俚】喝醉了：Call her a taxi, will you? She's **had one over the eight** and needs to go home. 可以給她叫輛計程車嗎？她喝醉了，現在要回家。

48. **a nine days' wonder**【英；舊】曇花一現或轟動一時的事物：People praised him to the skies, but he turned out to be **a nine days' wonder**. 他曾被捧上天，但那只是曇花一現。

49. **a stitch in time** (saves nine) 及時縫上一針可免將來縫九針；防微杜漸；小洞不補，大洞吃苦；及時處理，事半功倍：The sooner you see a doctor, the sooner you can be on the way to recovery. It's a case of **a stitch in time**. 早點看醫生，你的病情才會好轉過來的。正所謂病向淺中醫。

50. **dressed to the nines**【非正式】穿着盛裝；衣着時髦華麗：She likes to be **dressed to the nines** in order to impress people. 她在衣着上十分講究，希望這樣能給別人留下深刻印象。

51. **nine to five** 朝九晚五（的工作時間）：He's tired of working **nine to five**. 他厭倦了朝九晚五的上班時間。

52. **nine-to-five job** 朝九晚五的工作：He's tired of working freelance and wants a **nine-to-five job**. 他厭倦了打散工，想找一份朝九晚五的工作。

53. **nine times out of ten** 十之八九；幾乎總是：**Nine times out of ten** children will choose a hamburger rather than dim sum. 幾乎所有孩子都會選漢堡包，不選點心。

54. **on cloud nine** 歡天喜地；樂不可支；喜不自勝：When I won the Mark Six lottery, I was **on cloud nine**. 我中了六合彩，高興得不得了。

55. **Number Ten** 英國首相官邸（即唐寧街 10 號）：The front door of **Number Ten** is a steel plate. 唐寧街 10 號的大門是一塊鋼板。

56. **ten to one** 大有可能；十之八九：**Ten to one** he won't come to our party tonight. 他多半也不會來參加我們今晚的派對。

四）eleven to ninety-nine

57. **at the eleventh hour** 【喻】最後一刻：He always handed in his work **at the eleventh hour**. 他總是在最後關頭才交功課。

58. **talk nineteen to the dozen** 聊個沒完；喋喋不休：Whenever I get together with Kelly, we always **talk nineteen to the dozen**. 我每次跟凱莉見面時總是喋喋不休的聊個沒完。

59. **your daily dozen** 【喻】（每天做的）健身操：I always feel better after **my daily dozen**. 每天做一點運動，感覺多好。

60. **Catch-22** 左右為難；進退維谷：It's a **Catch-22** situation. 這是個無法擺脫的困境。

61. **forty winks** （在白天）打盹，小睡片刻：I need **forty winks** before I leave. 我離開前要睡一會。

62. **fifty-fifty** 平攤（費用）：We decided to split the money **fifty-fifty**. 我們決定把錢攤分，每人拿一半。

63. **ninety-nine times out of a hundred** 十之八九 (= nine times out of ten)；幾乎總是：**Ninety-nine times out of a hundred** I feel great, but sometimes I have emotional problems. 我總是心情開朗，但也有情緒困擾的時候。

五）one hundred and above

64. **a hundred to one shot / chance** 成功機會渺茫：She only has **a hundred to one shot** at getting into the university that she has hoped for. 她能成功考進她心儀的大學的機會很渺茫。

65. **a hundred percent** 百分之百；完全：I'm **a hundred percent** sure he has lied. 我非常肯定他有說謊。

66. **give a hundred percent** 竭盡全力：Everyone **gave a hundred percent**. 所有人都盡了全力。

67. **a chance in a million / a million to one** 幾乎不可能；百萬分之一（的機會）：It was **a chance in a million** that we could find the lost girl. 我們能找到那名失蹤女孩的機會微乎其微。

68. **your number comes up** 中彩了；好運來了：Bravo! **Your number came up**. 太好了！你的號碼中了！

69. **your number is up**【非正式】某人將遭殃、受罰;某人將厄運臨頭或死期
已到:He didn't mind taking risks because he knew **his number was up**.
他不介意冒險,因為他知道自己的時間已到。/ The shark swam towards
me and I thought my number was up. 那條鯊魚游過來,我知道我必死無
疑了。

I.

1. Sixty-seven 2. Two hundred and forty-three 3. Eight hundred and twenty-eight 4. One thousand seven hundred and five 5. Seven thousand and six 6. Forty-nine thousand two hundred and twenty 7. One hundred and fifty-three thousand, six hundred and ten 8. Two million, two hundred and twenty-five thousand, five hundred and twenty-five 9. Sixty-four million, eight hundred thousand, nine hundred and thirty 10. Three billion, five hundred and seventy million, nine hundred and eighty-four thousand, two hundred and sixty-one

II.

1. 56 2. 322 3. 969 4. 1,111 5. 8,088 6. 72,541 7. 121,302 8. 3,620,307 9. 11,100,101 10. 5,608,242,612

III.

1. Third 2. Twenty-second 3. Fortieth 4. Eighty-third 5. Ninetieth 6. A / One hundredth 7. Three hundred and sixty-first 8. Twenty thousandth 9. Forty-four million, three hundred and thirty-three thousand, two hundred and twenty-second 10. Seven hundred millionth

IV.

1. III 2. XXII 3. XL 4. LXXXIII 5. XC 6. C 7. CCCLXI

8. MCMXCVII 9. MMXIV 10. MMMDXXXV

V.

1. 7 2. 37 3. 55 4. 69 5. 92 6. 130 7. 400 8. 523 9. 2,000 10. 3,999

VI.

1. a half / one half 2. a third / one third 3. sixteen and a quarter / one fourth 4. thirty-three and three eights / three over eight

5. Seventy-five and one ninth

VII.

1. $^1/_5$ 2. $6^1/_{10}$ 3. $9^3/_4$ 4. $15^1/_9$ 5. $36^2/_3$

VIII.

1. zero point five 2. zero point zero two five 3. Four point six two eight
4. ninety-nine point nine 5. a /one hundred and thirty-seven point zero two 6. zero point six three percent 7. nine percent
8. nineteen point three four percent 9. a /one hundred percent
10. a /one hundred and fifty percent

IX.

1. Nine and nine is / are eighteen.

2. One hundred and twenty-five plus three hundred and forty-three is / equals four hundred and sixty-eight.

3. Six from thirteen leaves / is seven. OR Thirteen take away six leaves / is seven.

4. Six hundred and ninety-six minus two hundred and thirty-two equals four hundred and sixty-four.

5. Seven threes are twenty-one.

6. Twenty-four times two hundred and twenty is / makes five thousand two hundred and eighty. OR Twenty-four multiplied by two hundred and twenty equals five thousand two hundred and eighty.

7. Twenty-four divided by six equals four. OR Six into twenty-four goes four.

8. One thousand six hundred and sixty-four divided by thirteen equals one hundred and twenty-eight.

X.

1. three double seven double nine double three two / three double seven nine, nine double three two

2. six triple nine double eight zero (oh) one

3. three zero (oh) eight seven, seven zero (oh) six five, five two double oh (zero), eight triple oh (zero) / oh oh oh

SECTION 3: INTEGRATED SENTENCE EXERCISES 綜合句子練習

I.

    1. A 2. C 3. A 4. B 5. C 6. B 7. B 8. C 9. B 10. C, B

II.

1. Is it good to give solid food to babies under six months of age?

2. A woman aged / ages 60 has given birth to twins.

3. Girl ages between 13 and 18 are most at risk from sexual harassment.

4. He died at age ninety / at the age of ninety.

5. This temple was more than one hundred and fifty years ago.

6. She became a professor at the age of / at age twenty-seven.

7. There are thirty-three (or:33) ten-year-olds in this class.

8. She came third in Maths.

9. He has spent several million dollars on this sports car.

10. She was born on 8th July, 1992.

III.

1. I usually get up at eight in the morning.

2. She's 5 feet 2 inches (tall).

3. She weighs 48 kg (forty-eight kg / kilograms).

4. Victoria Peak is 552 metres high.

5. He got 83 marks out of 100 for science. / He got 83 percent in science.

6. She won the first set eleven seven (11-7).

7. She swam for her school in the women's 200 m (two hundred metres) freestyle.

8. I will run the men's 200 m (two hundred metres) hurdles.

9. You'd better finish your homework within one and a fourth / quarter hours.

10. Hong Kong has a population of 7.2 million.

11. They fell in love at first sight.

12. Liu Bang became the first emperor of the Han Dynasty (206 BC – 220 AD).

13. Water freezes at 0 degree Celsius / 0℃.

14. The bedroom is 120 square feet in area.

15. The latitude and longitude of Hong Kong is: 22° 15′ 0″ N / 114° 10′ 0″ E (22 degrees 15 minutes 0 second NORTH and 114 degrees 10 minutes 0 second East).

SECTION 4: INTEGRATED CONTEXTUAL EXERCISES 綜合篇章練習

I.

1. 25 2. Room 1603 3. 16/F 4. 2013 5. XXXIV 6. 250 7. One-litre

II.

1. A 2. A 3. B 4. A 5. C 6. A 7. B 8. C

III.

1. A 2. C 3. B 4. A 5. A 6. C 7. B 8. B

IV.

Witnesses of a UFO crash

It was late in the day, just before 1.(five) o'clock in the afternoon, on 2.(5) December 1965, when a fireball flashed through the evening sky. It was seen 3.(first) over Canada, then by 4.(thousands) in Michigan and Ohio. Over the northern edge of Ohio, near Cleveland, it might have made a slight turn, and then it headed southeast, towards Pennsylvania.

At 5.(4:47) P.M., the object struck the ground southeast of Pittsburg, near the small town of Kecksburg. In its wake it had left thousands of stunned witnesses, and debris reported to have fallen from it started fires near Elyria, Ohio.

Frances Kalp was interviewed for the breaking story of the object. She told the news director that the object had crashed into the woods near her home. Her children wanted to walk down to where her son said he'd seen 'a star on fire.' Kalp caught the children about one and a **6.**(half) mile from the crash site. There was smoke climbing out of the trees, and there was a bright object off to **7.**(one) side. Kalp said that it was like "a **8.**(four-)pointed star."

But Kalp was not the only person to see the object in the air. Bob Blystone, who was **9.**(fifteen) in 1965, saw what he described as an orange jet trail at low altitude. He drove down to the Kecksburg area. He was there when **10.**(two) state police cars arrived.

IV.

The Titanic

It's been **1.**(100 years / one hundred years) since the Titanic sank on its maiden voyage.

After the sinking of the Titanic on **2.**(April 15, 1912), the great ship slumbered on the floor of the Atlantic Ocean for over 70 years before its wreckage was discovered. On September 1, 1985, a joint American-French expedition, headed by famous American oceanographer Dr. Robert Ballard, found the *Titanic* over two miles below the ocean's surface by using an unmanned submersible called *Argo*. This discovery gave new meaning to the *Titanic's* sinking and gave birth to new dreams in ocean exploration.

Built in Ireland from **3.**(1909) to **4.**(1912) on behalf of the British-owned White Star Line, the *Titanic* officially left its final European port of Queenstown, Ireland on April 11, 1912. Carrying over **5.**(2,200) passengers and crew, the *Titanic* began its maiden voyage across the Atlantic, headed for New York.

The *Titanic* carried passengers from all walks of life. Tickets were sold to first, **6.**(second), and third class passengers; the latter group largely consisting of immigrants seeking a better life.

Only three days after setting sail, the *Titanic* struck the iceberg at **7.**(11:40) p.m. on **8.**(April 14, 1912), somewhere in the North Atlantic. Although it took the ship over two and **9.**(a half) hours to sink, the vast majority of the crew and passengers perished due to a significant lack of lifeboats and improper use of those that did exist. The lifeboats could have held over 1,100 people, but only **10.**(705) people were saved; nearly 1,500 perished the night the *Titanic* sank.

Section 5: Creative Writing Exercises 創意寫作

(Suggested Answers)

Ex 1: Jupiter is the fifth planet from the Sun in the solar system. It has a diameter of 142,984 km at its equator. Its atmosphere is approximately 75% hydrogen and 24% helium by mass. It has at least 67 moons, including the four large ones discovered by Galileo Galilei in 1610.

Ex 2: When she was in her teens, Great-grandma moved to Hong Kong from China. She got married when she was only 16. Her husband died in a war which broke out in the forties. It is Great-grandma's 88th birthday today. In her eighties, she is still very active and strong.

Ex 3: About one tenth of my classmates are new immigrants. Xiaoming is one of them. He always likes to sit in the first row. He often comes first in Putonghua. He got 99 percent in the last test. Xiaoming likes sports. He holds the school record for the men's 200m hurdles.

Ex 4: The king cobra is the largest venomous snake in the world. It can grow to as long as 18 feet. It sheds 4 to 6 times per year. It may live up to 20 years. A single bite from a king cobra is enough to kill 20 grown men.